ARCADIS: WAR!

BOOK TWO

Thank You for buying my
2ⁿᵈ book! Please read and let
me Know what You think about the
ongoing saga of Arcadis's Phlight!

George Kramer

By

George Kramer

DEDICATION

There are a few people I would like to dedicate this book to. First and foremost are my wife and daughter. Without their love, support, and patience, this book (along with the others) would not have been possible.

Thank you for my two beta readers, Anastasia Bayetakes and Ray Wininger. Your suggestions and feedback are always welcomed.

Thank you Greg Hebert for the great picture you took of me in the cold whilst I had the flu. Your guidance and skill with the camera are greatly appreciated!

Thanks to the illustrator, Courtney Monroe, for taking out time with her busy schedule to help me out!

Praise for the first Arcadis book:

Arcadis: Prophecy

"What a great read! The vivid imagery and captivating story really captures your attention and sucks you in to Arcadis' crazy, new world." *Anastasia Bayetakes*

"I read this book straight through and finished it the first day I got it. Never put it down once I started reading. Easily the most entertaining quick read I have read in the past year or so. I hope this author puts out more of these soon." *Adam Flora*

CHAPTER ONE

An infirmary isn't what one would expect in a magical world. There weren't any gadgets or electrodes affixed to your body. Needles, blood draws, anesthesia, blood pressure cuffs, stethoscopes and the whole gambit of medical devices and machines were non-existent. Sure, there was an assortment of beds which accommodated anyone's size, and there were nurses and doctors that check on your condition, but that's where the similarities ended.

I am Arcadis Ander Gildeon, a sorcerer. I have just been through hell and back when a friend of mine showed up at my antique shop bleeding all over my floor. I used my red primary magic to transport us to the infirmary, which was housed on the main floor of the Convocation. I looked around and most of the beds were occupied. When I probed my friend, Topec, I found to my amazement, there was a war being waged between the primary colored powered beings, which were red, blue and yellow colors, and the secondary or diluted powers. Jackson was leading the revolt. The purple powered sorcerer, Jackson, sliced Topec's arm when he refused to join the conflict. Topec was a Regulator. A simple comparison would be a policeman in the regular world. He and the remaining thirty-seven out of one hundred Regulators from the United States were of secondary power, but they swore allegiance to the three primary powered beings that comprised the Convocation. The most senior member on the board was my mother, who was red powered.

I looked around the sickbay and found an unoccupied bed. I gently placed Topec on it. His African American face was contorted with pain and his bald head was dripping with sweat. I called out to a nurse and she rushed over. I noticed her nametag said Ciana. She was wearing a blue nurse's uniform which indicated she was of primary power.

After my trial, orchestrated by my sister I did not know, there were more and more primaries who now were willing to help in the cause. My mother explained to me that the other two primary powered Convocation members - Arrake, who was blue primary powered and Garnom, who was yellow powered - had conspired to produce more primary powered beings after the death of Lord Quill thirty years ago.

"Ciana, my friend was stabbed by Jackson, the instigator of this war. Can you do anything for him?"

Ciana was shorter than I with long black hair that was tied tight and lifted under her blue nurse's hat. Her blue uniform fit snug, went past her knees and matched her eyes. She glanced at me and noticed my red trench coat.

"Your're red primary?" she inquired. Her voice was

smooth and pleasant.

I nodded. She bent down and looked into Topec's brown eyes. "He has lost a lot of blood. He'll need the healer scan. He's a gold power?"

Again I nodded. She was stating the obvious. Topec wore a gold colored trench coat.

She looked him over and mulled. "Since gold is an offshoot of yellow, I will have to place him under a low powered yellow healer scan."

I crossed my arms over my chest. It's something I do when I am being stubborn or want more information. "Please explain what that means and what that will entail."

Ciana's face changed. She became more rigid in her stance. "And who are you in relation to this patient?"

Just when I thought things were going right, I get a sanctimonious nurse. "I am his friend. Recently, we were in two major battles together."

She walked up to me so close I could see my reflection in her dark blue eyes. "I don't care if you were or not, he needs medical attention and not your interference. Now, if you would just leave..." Ciana gasped. She looked beyond me. I turned to see what made her stop talking. I noticed my mother walking in and was heading our way. My mother strode up to us and stopped. Ciana bowed all the way down and I did the same. Ciana was beside herself. "Madame Gildeon, what an honor for you to be here, especially after what happened in the assembly room!"

The assembly room, where my trial was. What an ordeal that was! We were all lucky to get out alive thanks to my sister who devised the whole thing.

"Thank you, Ciana. How is Topec doing?"

Ciana turned toward Topec and appraised him. "He lost a lot of blood. Since he is gold, I was going to place him in a low level yellow healer scan but" she pointed to me, "this pushy gentleman here was interrupting me."

My mother smiled. She was doing that more and more recently despite the ongoing conflict. "You'll have to forgive my son, Ciana. Arcadis is very protective of his friends."

Ciana's disposition changed immediately. She eye-balled me. "You're... you're Arcadis? *The son of the all powerful Lord Quill?*"

I smiled. "Yup, that's me. I guess my five-foot-seven, one-hundred and seventy pound frame doesn't instill much fear."

Ciana was embarrassed. Her creamy white complexion grew a few shades darker. "I am so, so sorry, Sir!" She bowed deeply to me and I returned the gesture.

"After you hook Topec up to the healer scan, can you please explain to me the process?" I asked nicely.

Ciana was beside herself. "Of course, Sir. I will get to it immediately!" She went to Topec's bed and started working on the quantum magical computer that was stationed beside Topec.

While she was attending to Topec, it gave me a chance to speak to my mother. I had not seen her since my trial in which we found out she was being influenced by my sister to have me killed. "How are you, Mother?"

She gave a warm smile. It was still hard to see her being nice to me. After so many years of her belittling me, I was still waiting for her to revert back. "I am doing much better, thanks to you." Her grey hair was pulled up with bobby pins. People still used those archaic products? She was still a little frail after having been forced by my sister to sum up her entire power to bring forth a monstrosity Lord Quill had created called the enchanted assassin. Arrake and Garnom, the other members of the Convocation, were forced to help her by their offspring as well.

"I waited over a week for Topec to show up to begin

my training as a Regulator," I said to fill in the silence.

"Why didn't you call him?"

I shrugged. "A Regulator is busy. I figured he was doing Regulator stuff."

My mother was quiet for a moment."Arcadis, did you foresee the secondaries uprising?"

I became reflective as I used my fingers to brush through my short hair. "No. I knew Jackson was mad over the handling of the trial and the aftermath. But, if he were fostering resentment, then he must have felt that way for a long time. I guess the circumstances were right for him to voice his concern." I heard a noise and looked to find the source. Topec's bed was bathed in a light yellow colored stream. The lights above him were going from his head to his feet and back again. It was slow and deliberate. My mother and I walked to the bed while Ciana was looking at a dial. I noticed an outline of his body was on the monitor. I could see his organs.

"Well Son, I have an important meeting to attend. I will see you soon." She came to me and hugged me. I could feel her centuries-old bony back. She bowed to Ciana who bowed back. I watched my mother leave and then turned to the nurse. She was playing with a dial.

"What's that knob you're fidgeting with?"

She continued looking at the switch and making adjustments. "If I move the dial to the right it increases the yellow power and conversely, to the left is lowering the yellow power." She played with it for another second and seemed satisfied. She walked past Topec and stood in front of me. "I sincerely apologize for my actions, Arcadis. Had I known who you were..."

I put up my hand. "Don't worry about it. It happens all the time to me. You kind of get used to it."

Ciana smiled. I noticed she had white teeth. She seemed unsure of what to say next.

"Would you mind explaining the healer scan to me?"

I asked.

Ciana's face became serious. "Let me check my patients and I'll be back momentarily. Is that okay, Sir?"

"Of course. Please call me Arcadis."

She giggled like a school girl and left. I walked around Topec's area. There were three more sorcerers on beds similar to Topec's. Two people were bathed in red, and the other one in blue. I did a rough count of empty beds versus beds that were filled. The ratio was dwindling. Since my arrival, I had noticed more and more people coming in for treatments. In my peripheral vision, I saw a glimmer of something move toward me. I whirled around quickly and latched onto someone's coat. It was Roan and his orange trench coat greeted me with wariness. "Hold on partner, I'm on your side!" I let him go.

"What are you doing here, Roan?"

Roan pointed to Topec's bed. "I wanted to see how Topec was doing. Damn treachery by Jackson, if you ask me."

I nodded. "How goes the battle?"

Roan sized me up. "There are only several hundred primaries versus several thousands of secondaries that have been incited, excluding the Regulators of course, how do you *think* it's going? Poorly. Speaking of which, why aren't you joining the battle? We could sure use your power!"

"Because, as of half an hour ago, I had no idea we were at war. When Topec showed up at my store all cut up, I probed him. That's the only way I found out. If there are several thousands of secondaries fighting us, what about the other population of secondaries?"

"Most are indifferent, they don't care. Some have joined our ranks. We're getting more and more recruits daily."

"Okay, good! To answer your question, I have every intention of helping after I make sure Topec is okay.

17

Where can I find you?" I asked.

"At your mother's office. She is in a meeting now, coordinating. She has fought alongside us the past couple of days. Wow is she powerful!" Roan looked beyond me. I followed his gaze. Ciana came back. "How is Topec, Nurse?" asked Roan.

"He'll make it, he just needs some time to recuperate."

Roan started to leave and stopped. "I'm glad everything worked out for you, Arcadis. The trial was bogus, so were the charges. Man, did you kick some ass with the enchanted assassin!" He bowed and I returned the gesture. He left me alone with Nurse Beautiful.

"Those stories are already becoming legend. So are you, Arcadis."

I was uncomfortable with praise so I changed the subject. "So, how does all of this work?"

"Well, to begin with, Topec is gold powered, which

is in the yellow family. We had found, much to our amazement, when a sorcerer was bathed in a light that represents his or her primary colored power base, it actually healed the person."

"How did you draw those conclusions?"

"Hmm, let's see. Do you recall the Plight of Lord Quill?"

"Yes, it was back in 1665 when Lord Quill was negotiating a peace treaty with the warlocks and the wizards in Berlin, I think. What about it?"

Ciana ushered me to follow her. We walked to the nurses' station and sat down. I took off my red trench coat and the coat returned to its original color, black. I placed it on the back of my chair.

"The official version was Lord Quill grew sick and had to come back home after the treaty was signed," I said. "What about it? He got better. It's required reading in school."

Ciana grew quiet. "In the medical field, rumors abound about incidents which pertain to my profession. I'm sure that's the way it is in most cases. However, there is side note to the story. When Lord Quill came back, he was almost completely drained of power. There wasn't the medical sophistication we have today. So, Arcadis, how did Lord Quill regain his power?"

"In the story I read, he slept for three days. When he awoke, he was at full power."

A doctor walked by with another nurse. They ignored us. I could see why. Another person came in with severe lacerations to her face. War wasn't pretty.

"That's the textbook version. Another version I heard through the medical grapevine was Lord Quill was poisoned by either the representative of the warlock or the wizard council."

I had to smile. "Even if that were the case, Ciana, how, according to your story, did Lord Quill heal?"

"I see you don't believe me, and that's fine. Lord Quill was saved by your grandmother."

I scoffed. Never in a billion years did anything like that remotely happen. "Where did you get that preposterous information? It would have been scandalous back in the day. A woman helping Lord Quill, and him allowing it? Are you sure we're talking about the same Lord Quill?"

Ciana put her hand up to shut me up. One of her veins on her forehead was protruding. "It's not as farfetched as you would think, Arcadis."

I laid out my hands. "Please, enlighten me."

Ciana looked around. "I don't have much time. I'll have to give you the condensed version." She took a deep breath and continued. "In 1665 Lord Quill barely made it back from the clandestine meeting. What was usually an easy trip became arduous due to his decreased power. Suffice to say, the details are sketchy. Four hundred and fifty years ago the world was a lot different. Lord Quill's rule was absolute. There was no Convocation, the primaries were in hiding, the secondaries were everywhere. Lord Quill went to his abode and did sleep for three days. That much of the story remains true." She looked at me for confirmation and continued. "Unbeknownst to him, one of his mistresses, a red primary, saw what terrible condition Lord Quill was in. She took his hand and willed her magic into him. For three solid days she stayed by his bedside. When he awoke, his power had returned to normal and your grandmother passed away. It was latter speculated she absorbed the poison from him and gave him her magic. It was akin to a blood transfusion for lack of a better term. That information was the inception of the healer scan."

"So... Why haven't I been told this if it's true?"

Ciana's blue eyes darted back and forth. "There are a lot of secrets still kept from you, Arcadis. Nothing is as it seems."

I frowned. "Funny, when I was in prison, a friend of mine said the same thing."

Ciana looked me over. She changed the subject. "It seems you've had an altercation. Your nose is a little off. Let me feel it."

I allowed her to touch it. I flinched when she pressed on it. "What happened?"

I had to dredge up the memory for her. "The enchanted assassin caught me off guard. He managed to punch me through my hastily applied shield and through my arms protecting myself. He packs a wallop. I barely survived."

She smiled. "You're amazing! You went up against the doomsday manifestation and survived."

I smiled sheepishly. "Yes, yes I did."

She was silent for a moment. "Did you want to go under the healer scan to fix your nose?"

"No thanks, there's no time. I did have more questions for you."

She looked at her watch. "Okay."

"Topec is gold powered so naturally a yellow healer scan works. What about a green or orange powered person? They are composed of two different primary powered colors too."

Ciana swiveled in her chair while she spoke. Her blue uniform hugged her body and it was difficult for me to stop staring. "Good question. Let's take a green secondary for an example. Since green is derived from blue and yellow, we have to analyze him or her first."

I leaned forward. "How is that accomplished?"

I think Ciana was enjoying the attention or was enjoying me. "We put the person on the bed just like Topec's, but we don't turn on any of the primary colors yet. We have a neutral color, or soft white, that scans the being. The soft white scans until it determines what

24

percentage they are."

I was confused. "Percentage of what?"

"What percentage of blue and yellow they are."

I folded my chest. "I am afraid I still don't understand."

She gave a warm smile and I saw her perfectly shaped white teeth. "All secondaries aren't fifty percent one color and fifty percent another color."

I was taken aback. "Seriously? I guess I never really thought about that before. It would make sense since children display characteristics of one parent over another."

"Exactly. It comes to genetics. So, if the person has more yellow than blue, we use the yellow light and vice versa."

"Was there ever a time when a person had more yellow than blue but the yellow healer scan didn't work and you had to use the blue scan?"

"My, you're a perceptive person, aren't you? Yes, it's rare, but it does happen. Generally we wait a couple of hours to see if there is any progress. If there isn't, we use the other color."

I was intrigued. "What sort of percentages typically make up a secondary?"

Ciana thought about it for a second. "The percentage varies greatly. For arguments sake let's use green again. It could be anywhere from fifty point one percent to rare cases of eighty to ninety percent one color over another, yet they still maintain the green colored power."

"What about Topec? He's gold. That's an unusual color for a sorcerer. As far as I know, he is the only one I had ever met with that color."

She looked over at Topec lying on the table. The soft yellow light was methodically going up and down his body. "He is certainly an enigma in the magical world. To be a gold- power, it can take three colors and not the average two that creates a secondary. There are a myriad of ways to produce gold but-" she turned to the healer scan and nodded, "Topec's genetic makeup suggests he is made from yellow, magenta, and blue. How the heck magenta showed up, I don't know. Somewhere in his lineage there must be a recessive gene or some other anomaly which did not show up until he was born."

"Interesting. Thanks for the information." Ciana looked at her watch and got up from her chair. I rose too. "One more question about Lord Quill and then I'll leave. Did they ever find out who poisoned him?" I asked.

Ciana shook her head no and walked away. At that point, I didn't know what to think. I walked back to Topec and watched the yellow power go back and forth for a few minutes. He'll be okay. Now, it was time for me to join the fight.

CHAPTER TWO

There are only a handful of things which get me mad. One of them is not to be told something, especially from your mother and it involved secrecy. I wanted to know if what Ciana told me was true. I walked out of the infirmary and headed straight for my mother's office. It felt as though I had walked two miles before I got to her receptionist. Phil, a loathsome pale blue powered being was sitting at his desk, looking at his fingernails. He didn't even look up when I approached him.

He had gray hair. Someone had to have put a bowl on the top of his head and cut around the bowl. I looked at his nails. He had picked them and they were bleeding.

"I have come to see Madame Gildeon." I tried to say it with authority so he would look up. He did not.

"Do you have an appointment?"

"No, do I need an appointment?" I asked with sarcasm.

Phil bit his fingernail, chewed it, spit out the nail, and it landed on the multi colored carpet.

He sighed as if talking to a young child. "Yes, you need an appointment. Madame Gildeon is a very busy and important lady."

"Well, I would really like to see her, *now*." I said the last word with emphasis. Didn't work.

"Yes, yes, I'm sure you have important business to discuss. How about I pretend to take your name and when you leave, discard the blank piece of paper?"

I almost laughed. Almost. "Phil, if you don't let me see my mother right now, I will use my power to make you go bald."

I didn't know if I could really do that, but it had the desired effect. He looked up and recognized me immediately. He stood straight up and when he did, all of the paperwork went flying off the desk. He tried to bow and grab the papers at the same time but was unsuccessful.

"For the love of Lord Quill, Arcadis! Why didn't you tell me who you were? Of course I will let your mother know you're here! Please, have a seat. Would you care for some coffee?"

"No, thanks. I'll just wait."

Phil grabbed the phone so hard I thought it was going to break. Was I that scary? If you went by looks alone, the answer would be a resounding no.

I sat down and read *'The Sorcerer's Journal'* about the latest news concerning the war. It was supposed to be an unbiased account. If what I read was any indication, the primaries were in trouble. We were simply outnumbered. Damn Lord Quill and his stupid decree.

I finished reading the journal and fell asleep. I don't know how much time had elapsed before I felt a gentle nudge. I opened one eye and saw Phil. He was standing inches from my face. I noticed he needed to pluck his nose hairs. "Yes, Phil?"

"Your mother, Madame Gildeon, will see you now, Sir."

I got up and bowed. He reciprocated. I walked by his desk and noticed he had picked up the papers. I knocked on my mother's office door. It was big and red colored. The grain in the enchanted wood was red too. I heard her yell for me to come in.

I opened the door and entered a spacious room. The first thirty feet was a light red carpet. When I passed the repulsive carpet, I saw my mother at her enormous desk. It was a red oak. She had a computer and five monitors, and she still had plenty of room. To her right there were huge pictures of Lord Quill from his youth until shortly before his death. On the left were pictures of the current members of the Convocation. Pretty bland, I mused. Seated in front of her desk were Arrake and Garnom.

All three of them bowed and I returned the bow.

"This is a surprise, Arcadis. I thought you would be tending to Topec," my mother said.

"He is in capable hands and there's nothing much I can do to help him. Except maybe to stay at his bedside, hold his hand for three days, and will my power into his to cure him, in case he was poisoned or something. Does that story ring a bell, Mother?"

I didn't think anything could startle my mother. Apparently I was wrong. It took her a second to recoup. Judging by her reaction, the nurse I had spoken to was dead on. Surprise, surprise.

Arrake and Garnom gave me a puzzling look which meant they weren't aware of the story. I wondered what stories they shared. It seemed to me they had no personality and let my mother do what she wanted. It was, luckily, none of my business.

"Arcadis, it seems people have been talking when

they shouldn't have." She said it with annoyance.

"So, it's true. Why am I always the last person to know anything around here?"

She turned to the two men. "Our business is done for now, Gentlemen. I expect both of you to join me in tomorrow's incursion."

We bowed and they left. My mother shot me a glance and sat down. I took a seat. She rubbed her face. Finally she looked at me and shook her head. "You know, if it were anyone else that did half the stuff you do, I would incinerate them. I mean it."

I smiled awkwardly. "I am who I am, Mother. It seems we have some history with Lord Quill that predates even you."

She stared at me for a second. "If I were to tell you every story concerning our family and the relationship to Lord Quill, you'd be fifty by the time I finished. I don't have time to tell you every nuance of every story,

Arcadis."

"I understand, really I do but..."

A thunderous explosion shook my mother's office. We both got up and ran to the door. I stood in front of her and peeked outside. There were scores of secondaries doing battle with some of the primaries. I saw some of them had taken Phil and were toying with him, pushing him from person to person. Nobody toys with Phil except me! I nonchalantly opened the door and walked to the crowd that held Phil. "Let Phil go, now!" I yelled. I know you're not supposed to use magic in the Convocation. I had already been charged with that at my trial, but I was not going to let anything happen while I was here. I targeted the two people that were pushing Phil and let them have it. I hit them in the chest and sent them flying. They fell hard to the ground. Silence ensued. People turned and looked. A wall of people separated as I walked through them to get to Phil. No one stopped me when I took him by the arm and led him away. So far, so good. I walked back to the crowd. "If it's a fight you want, let's go. You just pissed off the wrong person."

The crowd comprised about sixty people. All of them backed away, except one. Jackson. His glasses were taped together and his purple trench coat had seen better days. It was tattered in some places.

"Arcadis, what are you doing here?" he demanded.

I gave him a sneer as I walked up to him. I pointed a finger at his chest and hit him with it. "I was in the infirmary. Topec came to my shop and nearly died before I brought him here."

"Topec? What happened to Topec?"

"I probed him and I saw what you did to him. I don't take things like that lightly. You're a coward, Jackson." I let that sink in for a second. "How about you and I settle our score right here, right now?"

The secondaries formed a circle around me and Jackson. I noticed my mother allowed it because if she didn't, it wouldn't have happened.

Jackson stammered. He looked around fervently. "Arcadis, can't we come to some sort of agreement?"

I nodded but made damn sure he and everyone else in the room saw my fingers crackle with red magic. "Yes, you can give up this war, surrender or I will kick your ass. I am not allowed to kill you here or else that would be a viable option."

Jackson licked his dry, chapped lips and smiled. He turned around and faced the crowd. "See how the primaries are, everyone? They threaten us with their all-powerful magic! This is what I was talking about! This is what the war is all about. The inequality between the primaries and secondaries has to be stopped or you'll get people like Arcadis!"

Whoa, what just happened? He managed to turn the

situation around. He was good. "Nice try, Jackson. Don't make me out to be someone I'm not. Most, if not all of my friends are secondaries. I don't care what colored power you have. Yes, some of the laws are archaic, but fighting a war isn't the answer."

Jackson turned full circle to address everyone again. "See, even the son of Lord Quill admits the laws need to be changed!"

Things were getting from bad to worse. He was inciting the crowd. I would have to dissuade them before more fighting broke out. I looked at my mother. She looked like she was ready to jump in and do battle. Great. "Jackson, either leave now, peacefully or feel my wrath." I said it pure and simple but I meant every word. For emphasis I made sure he saw the pentagram on my chest start to turn red.

Jackson sensed his time was over. He walked backwards, never taking an eye off me. For that matter, I kept my eyes on him until the crowd left in the magical elevator someone had conjured up. Relief flooded through me.

Phil came rushing up to me and gave me a hug. I felt repulsed, but didn't show it. "Thank you, Arcadis! Thank you! You saved my life!" He bowed repeatedly.

I tuned him out. I needed to do some thinking.

"That was some performance, Arcadis," my mother said without conviction.

"I know. I really wanted to kick his butt for what he did to Topec, but I'm sure I'll get my chance soon enough," I said with regret.

"You seemed troubled, Son. What's the matter?"

I looked at her while rubbing my chin. "That was way too easy. I expected to do battle here."

She agreed. "I think Jackson wasn't expecting you here. You probably ruined his plans. With the addition of your power, he knew he couldn't inflict much damage."

"Yeah, that's probably it. Still, I think I should spend the night here, just in case. Do you have a spare room for me?"

"Of course, Dear. Phil, see to it that Arcadis has the best accommodations, understood?"

Phil bowed. "Of course, my liege. It would be an honor."

I checked my internal clock. It was close to ten at night and I was exhausted. I followed Phil to a spacious room with a king-sized bed, a closet the size of a bedroom with an array of clothes, shoes and ties. There was a dresser full of pajamas. I found one I liked. It had the emblem of Superman all over it. After all, Superman's emblem was red.

Phil waited patiently by the door.

"Yes, Phil?"

"Would you like some company?"

"No thanks, that's not my thing."

He sighed. "I meant female companionship."

"Oh... no. I am really tired and want to recharge my batteries."

"As you wish. Have a great night. And thanks again for saving me."

I smiled. "It was my pleasure."

After Phil left I put on my Superman pajamas and went to bed. And had the weirdest dream ever.

CHAPTER THREE

Did you ever have a dream that seemed so real it was surreal? I dreamt Ciana came into my room and slipped under the covers. I could actually feel her warmth. She nudged me to get closer yet I remained rigid in my spot. She laughed and poked me while slowly coming closer and closer. I saw my reflection in her eyes as she said, "Come and get me, Arcadis!" Somehow she managed to overrule my compulsion to flee. I felt compelled to go closer. Closer and closer I went until our lips touched and I could not hold myself back. We kissed with passion unlike I had ever felt before. I opened my eyes only to see blue mist where Ciana once lay. I awoke with a start. I bolted upright and looked around. No one was sleeping beside me. I willed a little magic into the room and sensed no one had come or gone during the night. How odd.

I got up only partly refreshed. I showered which seemed to help. I picked out a nice white collared shirt with dark blue pants. It's hard to match attire with a red trench coat. It would have gone better with the black trench coat I saw lying on the chair but once I donned my jacket, it would turn red.

I walked to the cafeteria and downed three strong cups of red powered coffee. I sat down at a nearby table that was empty. Glancing around, I noticed the room was practically empty. I checked my internal clock. Eight-thirty in the morning, where was everyone? Someone walked by and I tried to get their attention.

"Excuse me?"

The woman walked by a few feet before she realized I was talking to her.

"Me?"

"Yes, you. It's eight-thirty in the morning. Where is

everyone?"

She looked at her watch. It was yellow that matched her trench coat. "No, it's five-thirty in the morning. You need a new watch."

"That's impossible. My internal clock is never wrong."

The woman looked at me like I was nuts. Her wavy brown hair swayed back and forth as she walked to a table far away from me.

Normally if I were three minutes off I wouldn't be concerned. But three hours? Despite having three cups of red coffee, I decided to go back to bed. I set my internal alarm clock for three hours.

I closed my eyes and a second later, I woke up. Again, I checked my internal clock. It said eight-thirty. This time I dialed the operator and asked for the time. The voice activated machine said in a metallic voice it was eleven-thirty. What the hell was going on? I closed my eyes and willed my magic to fill the room. The pentagram that Lord Quill carved on my chest when I was three days old came to life and burned red. It burned through my Superman pajama top even though I didn't remember putting them back on. I willed the room to sense any wrongdoing that might account for my time trouble. Finally, I sensed a small residue of energy I hadn't detected earlier. I seized upon that energy. It tried backing away but I grasped it and willed it to the surface. The power was strong indeed, but not as strong as mine. The power radiated blue and a form started to take shape. The blue power tried in vain to escape but I wouldn't let it. I poured forth more magic and willed it to solidify so I could take a look at what was messing with me. After some time I recognized it. The blue colored power residue was Ciana. It was she who was messing with my head.

Anger filled me. And then, I woke up. Again. This

time my internal clock said eight-thirty and the operator confirmed it. Hopefully I put an end to her charades. I showered and got dressed for the third time even though technically it was my first time. I went back to the cafeteria and wondered if I really had the three cups of red powered coffee. I had another one just in case. I walked to the infirmary to see how Topec was doing and to put an end to Ciana's charade.

The infirmary had quieted down. Several of the sorcerers had gone home but others had arrived. I went to Topec's bed. The low powered yellow light was still going up and down his body but at least he was sitting up.

He bowed his head and I returned the gesture. "How are you feeling, Topec?"

His bald head creased as he smiled. "I am doing fine, my friend. You, on the other hand, look frazzled."

"Yeah, lack of sleep will do that to you." I looked at his light. "When are you going to be done with the treatment?"

"The doctor said I could leave soon." He turned serious. "I heard there was a disturbance here yesterday and it involved Jackson."

"He and a horde of secondaries came to wreak havoc."

Topec's brown eyes lit up. "And?"

"I don't think me being here was part of their equation. I backed Jackson into a corner for a fight but he wouldn't take my bait."

"Smart man. He would have lost."

I shuffled my feet. "Topec, I want to ask you something."

He looked me over and closed his eyes. "I know what you're going to ask me, Arcadis. My being a secondary and backing the primary, what do I really feel, whose allegiance do I really think is right." He opened his eyes. "Am I right?"

"Yes, but you didn't answer your own questions."

"I am a Regulator and I back the primary, period. I swore an oath. I will not break that promise."

I bent down to his ear. "Good, because I really didn't want to have to kill you." I smiled at him but he didn't return it.

I walked away and headed for the nurses' station. I saw Ciana doing paperwork. I snuck up to the desk. Her back was facing me. "Hey! What are you doing?" I screamed. Her paperwork went flying.

"Arcadis, you'll be the death of me!"

I placed my hands on the front desk. "Listen, Ciana, we need to talk."

Her blue eyes locked into mine. She knew that I knew. I wanted to probe her but then again I wanted the truth coming from her.

"I heard what happened yesterday and you saving the day."

So, she was trying to change the subject. I willed some magic and made her immobile in her chair. She noticed it at once and tried to free herself but couldn't.

"What are you doing, Arcadis? Are you crazy? Let me go or I'll tell your mother!"

I laughed. "That would've worked when I was a kid, but not now. I want some answers and I want them now."

She continued to squirm. "Arcadis, release me! I have work to do."

I looked down at her. "I could just probe you..."

She eyes shot back and forth. "No, don't you dare!"

"Why? Is there something you're not telling me?"

She struggled to free herself. Finally, she stopped. "Okay, you win. Release me and we'll talk."

"How do I know if I can trust you?"

"Look around you. We're in the Convocation, a sacred place. I am bound by my word here."

I released my spell. She got up, walked to the drinking foundation and sipped some water. When she came back she had a smile on her face.

"What's so funny?" I asked annoyed.

"It's so weird to have someone here as powerful as you. Sure, we have the members of the Convocation, but I rarely have contact with them. You were able to keep me seated despite me being a blue primary. Very few sorcerers would be able to do that to me."

I ignored her compliment. I wanted answers. "Is there some place we can talk more privately?"

"Sure." She walked around her desk and out through the back entrance door. I had never been to the back part of the Convocation. The hallways were less grandiose and smaller. The ceilings were lower. The hallway we were headed down had several paintings hanging on either side. I presumed most were of doctors and nurses who worked or had worked in the infirmary. The carpet was multicolored and hideous. Ciana went to a door marked conference room. We went in and I closed the door. For added security, I put a protection spell at the door. If someone was going to be barreling in, I wanted to know about it.

Ciana sat down and waited. I sensed nervousness. I stood for a moment and then took a seat next to hers. I looked at her and said, "What did you do to me last night?"

She wouldn't look at me. Not at first. "What are you talking about? Last night I was home alone."

"Ciana, you came to me in my dreams and then messed with my internal clock."

"How could you possibly have known? I have been doing that to a select group of people for over eight years and no one has ever remembered."

"Have you been doing it to primary and secondaries powers?"

"Yes, and not one person recalled anything. I usually

asked them the next morning if they remembered their dreams. Not one single person until you."

"How are you able to do it?" I asked with profound curiosity.

"It's a talent I developed since childhood."

"Well, don't do it to me again. If you wanted to be with me, all you had to do was ask."

"I had Phil ask if you wanted female companionship and you said no."

"If I had known it was you, it would have been a different story. Only Lord Quill knows what female creature Phil would have brought me."

She smiled. "Okay, next time I'll ask."

"By the way, why was my internal clock screwed up from your visit?"

"I don't know. You don't seem to operate like a normal sorcerer. It could have been a side effect. You're an enigma in the sorcerer's world."

"Thanks, I think. All right, I am going to coordinate with my mother. It's time I joined the battle."

"I hope I don't see you as a patient."

I grinned. "Let's hope not. I don't want to watch the red light cascade up and down my body. It would drive me nuts."

I released the protection spell and opened the door. I saw a secondary walk by and disappear into an unmarked room.

"Who was he?"

"He's a patient. There are different types of treatment rooms here."

The room grew quiet. I didn't have anything further to say. "Okay. I'll see you later."

"Let's hope so."

We parted ways. I started to walk back to the infirmary but turned around. I saw Ciana walk to one of the treatment rooms I saw the secondary enter.

When I arrived in the infirmary, Topec was putting on his olive trench coat and it turned gold the instant he put it on. Apparently what I had whispered to him earlier still resonated with him. He became the calm, cool and dispassionate person I remembered him as.

"You ready?" he asked as he put his gold sword in his coat.

I checked my red coat and nodded. We walked to my mother's office without speaking. When we arrived, the room was filled with Regulators, the members of the Convocation, secondaries which were on our side and several primaries of various colors. My mother had a couple of maps spread on her desk. I gently pushed my way through the crowd. I noticed one map was a topo-graphical and the other was a satellite map and it looked familiar.

"Mother, why do you have a map of Indiana? And more specifically, why one of McCordsville?"

My mother looked up. "Everyone, this is my son, Arcadis if you didn't know." I waved my hand in acknowledgement. "We had a breakthrough. We captured a few of Jackson's soldiers and we were able to extract this map from them."

"Why would they choose McCordsville of all places?" I asked in bafflement.

Arrake said, "We thought you could tell us."

I couldn't fathom why. "There's nothing there, except farmland, cattle, and crops."

"Then why do you live there, Arcadis?" said Garnom.

I looked at the yellow powered member of the Convocation. His tall frame was bent low looking at the map and looking at me. "I went there so no one would bug me."

He let out an exasperated sigh. "See how much good that did you."

True, he had me there. But what could be so important to Jackson? Nothing came to mind.

"Can I see the maps, Mother?" I bent down and took a look. There was a small, almost unseen dot on the satellite map. "Mother, do you have a magnifying glass?"

She reached into a drawer in her desk and pulled one out. It had a red handle, of course. I put the magnifying glass where I saw the dot. Color drained from my face.

"What's the matter, Arcadis?" My mother inquired.

I picked up the satellite map so everyone could see and pointed to the dot. "I saw a very small dot on the map the prisoners gave you. Using the magnifying glass, I discerned where Jackson is headed."

"And where might that be?" Topec bellowed from the back of the crowd.

"My antique shop."

CHAPTER FOUR

"**W**hy would Jackson go to your antique shop?" Roan asked. He had moved to the front of the room. His orange trench coat did not match the red interior of my mother's office.

"I have an idea but I want to verify it first. Mother, give me twenty minutes and I may have an answer for you."

"Proceed." I walked to the back of her office and Topec stopped me.

"Do you require assistance?"

I put my hand on his shoulder and he stiffened. "No, thanks. I'll be right back."

I raced out the door and headed to the prison unit. It took a few minutes to get there. At the beginning of the unit there stood a guard. He had the coolest staff I ever saw. It was long, made of enchanted metal, which was harder to come by than wood, and had a large quartz crystal on the tip of his staff. The crystal was held in place by three elongated metal branches which came from the sides of the staff.

He stopped me. I had to look up to see his face. He had to be six ten and weighed at least three hundred pounds of solid muscle. He had some scarring on his face, probably had acne when he was a child. His blond hair was cut like the military. He had nothing to indicate what power color he was. His uniform was off white.

"What do you want, Peanut?"

"Excuse me?" I asked with indignation.

He lowered his beefy head and glared at me. "Just because you're a primary doesn't mean you can waltz in here and demand anything you want, Peanut."

"I hadn't uttered a word, Jerk."

Obviously he hadn't expected to be challenged especially by someone as little as me. He raised his staff at my midsection. "Do you want to feel my power, red one?"

I really didn't have time, but he really bugged me. "Yes, yes I do."

He registered surprise, but quickly came to his senses. He shot out a blinding fast energy bolt. It had no color, which was weird, but I was able to see the blast head toward me. I moved away and shot him a red blast that sent him reeling. He stood unsteadily and seemed quite angry. He shot another bolt and that one hit me. I was knocked hard to the ground. The blast was incredibly powerful! I shook my head a few times to gain my composure. The blast tore a hole in my shirt which made me mad. I liked that shirt. I didn't have time to repair it magically. My pentagram on my chest turned dark red. I raised my hands and they crackled red magic. The guard saw the pentagram and backed up with his hands in the air. "Whoa, wait a sec. No one told me the son of Lord Quill was here. Sorry, I was just doing my job!"

"Your job is to harass people? And who said you could use magic in the Convocation?"

"I am sorry about the confusion, Sir! It won't happen again. I am allowed to use magic in case a prisoner escapes."

"I need to speak with my sister, Alay."

"Did your mother approve it? Only she can."

"She knows I am here. Do you want me to call her and tell her you attacked me?"

"No! That won't be necessary. You can see her. I'll get one of the guards to bring her in a magical free room. Will that be all, Sir?"

"Yes." I walked by him as he opened the locked door. I was glad they would put us in a magical free room. I would be able to talk to her, but her side would be magic free and mine would not. I would still have my power.

When I was in prison and lost my power, I hated every second of it. An added bonus was the magic bracelets I placed on her hands which negated her power too. By the time I reached the room Alay was sitting waiting for me. She still had the short blond hair and the superior attitude judging by her posture.

"Well, well, look who came to pay me a visit. My long lost brother."

I sat down and looked her over. "You're looking well, Alay. Your red prison uniform goes well with your complexion."

She snorted and turned away from me. An invisible wall separated us. I could feel the pulsating energy.

"What do you want Arcadis, to gloat?"

"I don't have time to gloat and even if I did, it's not in my nature to do so."

"Then what can this poor non-magical person do for you?"

I rolled my eyes. "Save me your self-pity. I came here to find out where the magic spell book is that you stole from our mother."

She suppressed a smile. "Why would I do something stupid like that?"

"Because it may help save thousands of lives."

She laughed and banged her fists on the table. "My goal was to kill millions of people, not thousands."

I said nothing and let the silence fill the room. After a minute or two, I spoke softly, confidently. "I know where the book of spells is, Alay."

"Then why come here and ask me?"

"I want confirmation."

She rolled her eyes. "Like that will happen."

I leaned toward her to the point of touching the invisible wall. "When you came to my shop the night Lucinda Bianca and I faced off, you had the book with you, didn't you? You had to make sure your plan would work. But you didn't count on Lord Quill coming out of my chest and defeating her, did you?" There it was! I saw something in her eyes that gave it away. "You hid the book somewhere in my antique shop, didn't you?"

"No, I did not."

It was my turn to laugh. "It was in front of my eyes the whole time! Thanks."

Her eyes turned to slits. "You'll never find the book, Arcadis. That I'm sure of."

I looked at her without any remorse. "Just like you were sure you would defeat the Convocation? Just like you were sure the enchanted assassin would defeat me? I will find the book, Alay."

"Do you know why I hate you so much, Arcadis?"

I shrugged."In all honesty, I don't."

"In all the years I worked hard, trained, perfected my magic, all you had to do was use the power Lord Quill gave you."

"It's not my fault Lord Quill had an outdated view of our genders. I personally think it was stupid. You were born first, you should have had the pentagram. However, that's not how life is, Alay. It is what it is."

"For the last couple of years all I ever heard was, 'Arcadis this Arcadis that'. It made me sick."

I had enough. I got up, started to walk away, and stopped. "I never even knew I had a sister until recently." And just to be a jerk I added- "By the way, when do you go for reconditioning?"

She gave me the middle finger, stood straight up and, stormed back into her unit.

I practically ran full speed back to my mother's office. The guard led me back through and saluted me. I would have to do something about him. His type of disposition didn't sit well with me.

When I got back to my mother's office, everyone had conjugated outside in the lobby of the Convocation. It was much bigger and could handle more people. More reinforcements arrived. I sought my mother and pulled her aside. I didn't want anyone to know about the book. If it ever fell into the wrong hands, like Jackson's, I don't know if the combined might of all the primaries power would be enough to stop him. I told her the spell book was located somewhere on the premises of my shop. "We need to take only members we trust, Mother. I don't want a sympathizer coming along with us, finding the book, and handing it over to Jackson."

"Agreed. Let's take a dozen of our most loyal people. We'll have the rest scout out a five- mile perimeter from your shop in all directions. Maybe they can capture some of his followers."

I agreed, but made sure Topec and Roan were with me. My mother looked at me. "By the way, what happened to your shirt?"

I looked at my shirt and the pentagram was clearly

visible. "I had a miscommunication with one of your prison guards."

"Was he tall and muscular?"

"That would be him. He called me peanut."

I could see my mother suppress a smile. "Mack. I'll deal with him later."

Within a few minutes of my mother barking out orders, everyone was ready.

Topec created a magical elevator for the dozen of us and one of the other Regulators conjured up a huge elevator for the rest of them. We entered and were on our way.

CHAPTER FIVE

The dozen of us entered my antique shop. It was one-thirty in the afternoon, but you wouldn't know it. All the drapes were closed which gave it the appearance of being nighttime. I walked a few feet and tripped over something. A lamp, one of the many things that fell when my mother tried to barge her way in when I had several of my protection spells up. I heard another noise and someone tripped over something and cursed. Topec came to me and hissed, "You never cleaned this place? We're making too much noise!"

I raised my hand and concentrated. I willed my magic to lift everything off the floor and placed them on the two ugly couches I had. It took precious seconds but it was worth it. I fumbled around in the dark. If Jackson was here, he would have attacked by now. I went to the wall switch and turned on the lights. The place was a mess. Well, usually it's a mess, but this was a little different. Things had been moved and smashed. So Jackson had been here. The other people in the room came to the same conclusion.

"We're too late," my mother stated.

I looked around. "Yes, but did he find the book of spells?"

Topec whispered in my ear. "Why don't you ask the Soul Trees?"

In my haste, I had forgotten about the Soul Trees. When I bought this place I put an enchantment up which caused the trees behind my store to become sentient. They are supposed to dole out advice; however, last time I needed them they were useless.

"The enchantment is no longer, so they are no longer alive in magical terms. They wouldn't be a good source of information." I walked to the back of the store and everyone followed me. I opened the door and we stepped outside to an ambush. "Duck!" was all I could muster in the scant seconds we had. They were various colored magic being thrown at us. I dove down, came back up, and shot four successive bolts to the people closest to me. They all went down but then came back up. How was that possible? I scurried over to my mother who was actively engaged in battle. The same thing was happening to the others. We were knocking them down which should have put them down permanently, but they kept coming back up. Topec was in the midst of a sword fight with a secondary. He sliced someone's arm but a second later, the arm on the person healed. How was that possible?

Someone shouted from the fifty or so people we were battling. "Stop, people! Stop!" the voice commanded. All the hostilities ceased. The crowd dispersed and out emerged Jackson.

He looked different than the last time I saw him. He no longer wore glasses and his violet trench coat looked brand new. He emanated raw power. I sensed his power was equal to or above mine. How was that possible while he still maintained the violet power?

Jackson walked up to me and smiled. "Looking for this?" he asked as he took the book of spells from his trench coat.

"Actually yes, I was looking for that. It belongs to the Convocation and not to you."

Jackson chuckled. "Yes, well we had a change of plans. With this book, I will be the Convocation."

I looked at him with deadpan eyes. "Do you know how many people have told me the same thing over the years? Please."

Jackson's demeanor changed. He looked at me and his eyes turned from blue to violet, the color of his power. "*Solvite!*" he yelled.

I knew what that word meant though I never used it in an incantation. It meant destroy. The violet energy smacked me squarely in my chest and sent me hurling. I slammed into the back wall of my antique shop full force. I wasn't prepared for the magnitude of his attack. I didn't have time to put up a shield. I went down but didn't try to get back up because I couldn't. I found myself glued to the spot and sensed I could move my hands, but only slightly. Wow! Even the enchanted assassin didn't hit me as hard. Then again, with him I had just enough time to put up a shield. The creature managed to break my nose. With Jackson, I may end up having more things broken.

Jackson and his friends came to where I was propped up against my shop. Blood dripped freely from my nose. I should have used the healer scan like Ciana suggested.

"Look at the almighty Arcadis everyone! Look how easily he was defeated!"

I looked at my surroundings. It was bad, very bad. Jackson's henchmen had the eleven people I was with, and every one of them had swords to their throats. Even the three senior members of the Convocation. You had to possess an awful amount of power to do that, or you needed an extremely powerful spell.

Jackson leaned down and punched me in the face. Great, first a bloody nose, now I'll have a black eye. Damn that hurt, but I refused to yell out in pain.

"What's the matter, Arcadis? Nothing funny or sarcastic to say?"

"Give me a minute and I'll think of something," I said with false bravado. I checked my hands. I still couldn't move them much. The problem with my magic was when I conjured up a spell, my chest always glowed red. That meant the person or persons knew I was going to discharge my magic. Usually that was a good thing, but not in this circumstance. I needed to free up my hands so

I could attack Jackson, but he would become aware of it the second my chest turned red. I still wore the burned shirt from the skirmish with the prison guard. My chest was exposed. Come to think of it, I will start wearing black shirts so it won't be as easy to discern when I'm about to attack someone, albeit that didn't help me now.

Jackson punched me in the face again. And again. I could feel one of my eyes shut.

"Stop hitting him!" my mother shouted.

Jackson looked at my mother and smiled. He conjured up a sword, turned around and put the edge of the blade to my throat. He went slowly from one part of my throat to the other. It was deep but not deep enough to kill me. Blood trickled from my nose and my throat. He stood confidently, and went to my mother. He slapped her hard across the face. My mother's gray hair became disheveled and I could see his hand imprint on her face.

"How dare you slap me! You will pay dearly for that,

Jackson!"

Jackson laughed. "What are you going to do about it, Madame Gildeon?" He walked to the center of the pack of people. "I proclaim the era of the Convocation officially over!" He hoisted the book in the air. His supporters cheered in unison.

I saw tears forming in my mother's eyes. I was losing blood but felt I had to do something, anything to stop Jackson. While Jackson was gloating and not paying attention to me, I willed magic to my hands. I was able to free them more. It wouldn't be long before Jackson turned his attention back to me. I willed my thoughts into my mother. *"Mother, you're close to Arrake and Garnom. Tell them to hold hands with you. Use your combined might and push Jackson over to me. I have a plan!"*

"They will notice, Son," she shot back.

"Just do it!" I commanded. *Geez, what a time to ar-*

gue with me!

I saw her close her eyes for just a second. But that was all that was needed. Jackson was still giving his election speech as the three of them held hands.

Jackson sensed something was wrong. He turned around and saw the three of them holding hands. "How pathetic, the three of you holding hands shortly before your deaths."

"Now, Mother!" I screamed out loud.

The three of them yelled out loud in unison. *"Oppugnare!"*

The combined force of the three primary magic assaulted Jackson. He was shoved by their united wills and fell down beside me. By that time my hands were free. Jackson looked at me and I at him. The book had fallen to the ground and it was between us. The spell had been broken. We both reached for the book of spells at the same time. I got to it first because Jackson took a second to figure out I could move. However, he grabbed the book too. It was a tug of war. Then something odd happened. The book enveloped my psyche. Jackson was thrown away, but not by me. The book did it. I know how crazy that sounds but it was true. The book of spells was apparently sentient. I guess in the magical kingdom anything was possible. I was thinking the book pre-ferred my primary magic to Jackson's secondary magic. Did it do the same thing to anyone who was enchanted and picked the most powerful person? And how was my mother able to put it down for thirty years and not crave the power that was coursing through me?

I screamed at the top of my lungs for an eternity. It wasn't from pain, it was from the sheer power I was being fed. Every spell, every counter spell, every incan-tation was being burned into my brain. I was on a magi-cal high. Finally, after several agonizing but pleasurable minutes, the book crumbled, the pages turned to dust and then everything went blank.

I regained consciousness but I was no longer at my antique shop. Instead, I was strapped to a bed similar to the one Topec had been on. I looked around and saw several people milling around. "How... did I get here?" I inquired.

People rushed to me. I saw Ciana, my mother, Topec, and Roan come to my side.

"We transported you here, Son. What is the last thing you remember?"

I peered at my mother. Jackson's hand imprint had faded but a glimmer of it remained. She managed to fix up her hair. "I remember... I remember having a tug of war with Jackson. The book of spells was firmly lodged in both our hands, then a sudden sensation unlike any I had ever felt before wrapped itself all around me... and then waking up here." My mother nervously glanced to Ciana. "What? What happened? Where's Jackson? Did the son of a bitch get away?" I asked with concern.

"You honestly don't recall what happened?" Topec asked with concern.

I stared at them and was puzzled by their expressions. "For the love of Lord Quill, tell me what happened!"

My mother pulled up a chair beside me. I tried to move but was bound to the bed. "Why am I restricted in my movements, Mother?"

"It was just a precaution, Dear. You see, while you were absorbing the book of spells, you were hollowing in bliss, at least that's how I would describe it. Before passing out you gazed at everyone and your eyes shot to Jackson. Pure red energy radiated out of your eyes and beams of that energy scorched Jackson where he stood. You vaporized him, Arcadis."

I let that information sink in. "What about the other secondary members of the resistance, what happened to them?"

"After you incinerated Jackson, no one wanted to mess with any of us and they surrendered without a fight," Roan boasted.

"I don't recall any of what I am being told. But I'm glad the resistance is over."

Topec came to me. "There are still pockets of fighting, but we'll deal with that issue later. Right now, Ciana has some... interesting news for you."

Ciana came forward. Topec and my mother moved out of her way. Her penetrating blue eyes bore into me. There was some puffiness under her eyes as though she had been crying. "Hi, Arcadis. I am sorry about your restraints. I believe it's okay for us to remove them. Doctor Shell, do you concur?"

A small man approached. He wore a yellow lab jacket with a badge. "MD" was written on it with his picture and name. He had a severe receding hairline with green beady eyes. His small mouth opened into a grin. I noticed he had yellowed and crooked teeth. "Yes, I think the danger has passed. He is not a harm to himself or to others." He turned around and left. So much for bedside manners.

Ciana opened my restraints and I rubbed my wrists. "So, what's the prognosis? Am I going to live?"

Ciana smiled and brushed my hair back with her hand. "Yes, but there's some information to soak up, are you ready?"

I looked at her, and everyone else, with dubiousness. "Am I going to like it?"

"Truthfully, I don't know. But let's start, shall we? First off, for some inexplicable reason no one here can ascertain, your bone density is now thirty-three percent thicker then yesterday. I was able to get your medical chart, courtesy of Madame Gildeon. I compared the x-ray's you had last year to the one today. No doubt about it. Secondly, you know have ten layers of skin versus seven layers like the rest of us, including humans. My only supposition is for protection, but I could be wrong."

"Wow, that's amazing. Well, time to get up and find the other members of the resistance."

I started to get up but Ciana gently forced me back down. "There's more, Arcadis. Stop being so hard-headed when I'm trying to explain medical stuff to you."

I put my hands up in submission. "Okay. What else? Isn't that enough?"

Ciana looked at me with a contorted smile. "You just absorbed the most powerful book on our realm, possibly on any realm, and all you want to do is Regulator stuff?" She shook her head in confusion. "One of the alterations is interesting. When I put the red powered healer scan on you, you registered sixty percent red, twenty percent blue, and twenty percent yellow."

"Impossible. Lord Quill and my mother were both

reds. There should only be a nominal amount of the other two colors."

"Nevertheless, the healer scan doesn't lie. Somehow the book gave you additional colored magic."

"Huh," was all I could muster.

"There are other changes to you, Arcadis. Madame Gildeon, can you get me my mirror on my desk, please?"

"Certainly." It took less than ten seconds for her to retrieve it. My mother handed the mirror to Ciana who handed it to me. I looked at myself and was stunned. My hair had turned red. Not the orange type you see with freckled people, but red like my magic. It was weird. Another thing I noticed was the color of my eyes. They too had turned red. I glanced at my skin and my epidermis had a slight red tinge to it. Now I'll never get any women! "What, in the name of Lord Quill, happened to me?" Now I was freaking out.

"Calm down, Arcadis. I did some non-invasive tests

and came to some preliminary conclusions. Your red colored power level has skyrocketed to a degree we can't configure with our current technology. If I had to give an educated guess, your power has easily quadrupled, maybe more. You are bursting with so much magical energy it has permeated your skin, your eyes and your hair. How this was done is beyond our current understanding."

I gazed at my mother. "Why didn't this happen to you, or to Jackson or Alay? All of you were in possession of the book."

My mother's diminutive frame shrugged while concern was etched on her face. "In all of our recorded history, Arcadis, nothing remotely resembling what happened to you has been recorded. I checked with all of the Chroniclers. I checked the quantum magical computers, nothing."

"Great. Anything else?"

"Yes. Your brain has grown, probably to accommodate all of the information you absorbed."

I touched my head frantically.

"Don't worry, your head didn't grow, just what's inside it," Ciana said with amusement.

"Wonderful. I was a freak before, now I'm a super freak."

My mother came to my side and touched my cheek. "Son, you were never a freak. You were given a gift, a very powerful gift when Lord Quill carved the pentagram on your chest. Now your gift has been augmented. Don't look at it in terms of freakiness. Do you know how many of us would jump at the chance of having that much power? I know I would!"

I didn't look at it like that. Maybe it would work out for the best. "Just how powerful am I, Ciana?"

She bit her thick lip and looked at my mother. "I can only hazard a guess. I would say you are now more powerful than the three senior members of the Convocation and the enchanted assassin combined."

"Wow! So, am I more powerful than even Lord Quill?"

"Hard to say since Lord Quill's power flows through you, but I think so."

"Don't let it get to your head, Arcadis," Topec said with a poker face.

I smiled. "I'm not, but I feel like a kid at a candy store with a billion dollars to spend."

"Good analogy, Son," my mother beamed.

The door to the infirmary opened. A Regulator named Aredous entered. If memory served me correctly, he was from the southern section of Illinois. He was my height and wore a green trench coat which denoted his colored power. He had jet black hair with dark brown eyes. He easily weighed two hundred and fifty pounds. Most of it came from his generous midsection. He took my mother to the side and whispered something in her ear. Her features froze. She nodded to him and they exchanged bows. She came back to us and sighed heavily.

"Well, I have some bad news. Alay escaped."

"What?" everyone said in unison.

"You remember the guard at the prison you had the fight with, Arcadis?"

"Yes, I think you said his name was Mack, what about him?" I asked warily.

"He took a liking to her. She seduced him and when he slept, she stole his staff, reduced him to ashes, and escaped."

"Mother, that staff was enchanted metal, not wood, and shot out clear magic. It knocked the snot of out me. Someone of his stature doesn't have access to clear magic or enchanted metal, it's too cost prohibitive for most people."

"What's the difference between enchanted wood and

enchanted metal?" Ciana asked.

"You can get enchanted wood at any magical store and fashion your staff to your specifications. Enchanted metal is a different ball game. Costs aside, it has to be enchanted and fashioned by an extremely powerful sorcerer. Not every primary can do it. And when you add the crystal I saw on the tip of his staff, it augments the power. Mother, I'm thinking there was more to Mack then we were led to believe."

"Okay, then what is clear magic? I never heard of it," Ciana said.

"Clear magic is void of color. It's neither primary nor secondary but is extremely powerful."

"I'm confused," Ciana said as she looked to me.

"Think of it this way. If there is no color to your magic, it can bypass, or go straight through any colored power, primary or secondary. It actually goes through the color of your magic when it is directed at you because the colored magic doesn't recognize it."

"And how do you know that, Arcadis?" Roan asked with growing suspicion.

I pointed to my head. "In the book of spells, there is a whole section devoted to the history of magic. I just accessed the part that was germane to our conversation."

"So, if Alay stole the clear magic staff..." Topec started.

"She can release the bracelets because the clear magic would bypass the colored magic, thus freeing her, and I presume her friends," I finished the sentence for Topec.

"Are there beings that possess clear magic?" Ciana asked.

"I don't think so. According to the records, there are only three known staffs that possess clear magic. They were forged for three different lieges."

"I know of only one liege, Lord Quill. Who are the other two?" Topec asked with skepticism.

"You forget we aren't the only magical beings. One was given to Lord Quill, the other to the King of the Wizards, Anala and the last one was given to the King of Warlocks, Eos."

"Who forged them, and why?" Roan asked.

"Toris did. He was the one that trained Lord Quill. It was stated Toris was so powerful in his dimension he accidentally created a wormhole that led to ours. Once he walked through, the wormhole collapsed. It was written Toris couldn't use his magic here to recreate another wormhole to get back to his realm because his dimension was so far removed from ours. Our reality was weaker in magic than his, he claimed."

"But that doesn't explain why he created the staffs," Ciana commented.

I stood up and stretched. I was sick of lying on the healer scan. I felt my face and it no longer hurt. Good. I brought a chair from the nursing station and planted myself next to my mother and Ciana. The rest preferred to stand.

"Toris searched our realm because he was drawn to Lord Quill's growing power. He surmised with Lord Quill's help, he could get back to his world. He found Lord Quill in England and they became friends. Lord Quill readily agreed to help Toris. However, Lord Quill's help wasn't altruistic. When he learned of a realm more magically powerful than ours, he wanted to go there to steal some of it and come back here. For three decades they worked alongside each other with no success. Toris' powers were slowly fading. Lord Quill became frantic. He knew he would never get to the other dimension so he devised a plan to steal Toris' remaining power."

I looked around and everyone was riveted so I continued. "Toris was no dummy. He realized what Lord Quill was up to. In 1665, when Lord Quill went to Berlin to sign a peace treaty with the wizards and warlocks, Toris used his remaining power and created the three clear magic staffs. The crystals on top of each staff were in his possession when he accidentally came to his realm."

Ciana spoke up. "So the magic Toris used was the clear magic? Makes sense."

"Yes. He secretly followed Lord Quill to Berlin. He left one of the staffs in England with a note to Lord Quill explaining everything. After Lord Quill became sick and left, Toris went to Anala and Eos and offered them the staffs as gifts. They readily accepted the gifts and parted ways. No one knows what happened to Toris, there are no records to indicate where he eventually died."

"How did a security guard manage to get hold of Lord Quill's staff? I didn't know Lord Quill even had one. And where are the other two?" my mother asked.

"I don't know how Mack was able to get his hands on it or how he even knew about it. I presume the other two are still with Anala and Eos," I said dubiously.

"Are they still alive? That was over four hundred and fifty years ago," Roan added.

"I believe so. Lord Quill was much older than the other two supreme rulers," I said.

My mother interjected. "How is it the book of spells is able to tell you this information when the Chroniclers knew nothing of this?"

"While the Chroniclers are magical *beings*, the book is *pure* magic. Every time a new spell is introduced, it is recorded in the book, or in my brain. Every time I access a part of the book, stories appear. The account of us defeating Lucinda is in there now, as are my trial and Alay's escape."

"Does your perception of the account influence the book's narrative?" my mother asked.

"I don't think so. The book of spells is magic in its purest form. I doubt it could be anything but unbiased."

A stillness ensued.

"What we have to do now is find Alay. Does anyone know how to do that? She can make herself disappear where I can't even detect her," my mother asked with concern.

"I know how we can find her, Mother. We can track her red magic."

"How?"

"Every colored powered being, regardless of their purity or hue, gives off a unique wavelength. I was with Alay long enough to know her signature. I can tune into that frequency."

Topec shook his head. "What can't you do, Arcadis?"

I gave a weak smile. "I don't know, but we can't worry about that now. Let's hope we can track her and take away the clear magic staff."

"When we get the staff, what happens to it?" Roan uttered.

"Magic like that should be in no one's hands, not even mine. We'll either destroy it or hide it where no one on this planet will be able to locate it. Do you agree, Mother? You're the most senior member of the Convocation. It's your call."

"I don't see any sense destroying it since there may still be two of them left. We may need it down the road. I propose we hide it."

"Good enough for me. The Convocation has spoken," I intoned. No one questioned my mother's judgment nor did I expect anyone to. Hands down, she was the law.

"Can you track her now, Arcadis? I'm itching for battle." For emphasis Roan brought up his sword which pulsated orange.

"Are you ready, Mother?"

"Yes, quite ready."

I closed my eyes and thought of Alay. I sensed her aura, her frequency, and her movements. It took less than three minutes. I opened my eyes. "I know where she is."

"Where?" demanded my mother.

"She is heading toward my antique shop. She is almost there."

"Why there? Why does everyone conjugate there?" Topec asked with surprise in his voice.

"It seems Alay doesn't know the book was found. She was in prison. We need to act fast."

"I'll conjure up an elevator," Roan offered.

"No time. We'll go my way." I opened my arms, my pentagram burned bright and I encased us in a red bubble and disappeared.

CHAPTER SIX

We arrived shortly before Alay did. I sense her nearby. The shop was still dark. We decided to keep it that way for the element of surprise.

I honestly did not know how I would fare against clear magic despite my augmentation of power. The clear magic came from a dimension far removed from my own. I didn't know if the laws of magic were applicable to clear magic. But I knew one thing. I was sure going to find out.

The front door to my shop blew open and Alay stepped in. So did her two friends, Shelby and Corey. Alay had her hand tightly gripped on the clear magical staff. She hadn't detected us yet. I used my increased power to enclose Shelby and Corey in a red bubble and quickly made the bubble spin around the shop. Faster and faster the spinning red bubble went. I wanted them out of commission. Alay noticed immediately. At first she tried her red magic to stop the spinning bubble but was unsuccessful. My mother shot a bolt of red lightening at her and Alay careened into a wall and fell. Alay staggered to her feet and blasted my mother using the clear magic staff. It hit my mother squarely in her chest. My mother went down and did not come back up. Topec came and swung his gold sword at Alay who deflected it with her staff. She aimed her staff and shot it. Thankfully Topec was fast enough to get out of the way. Roan came from behind her and managed to lacerate Alay's back. She howled in pain, swung around, and hit Roan full force with a blast of pure clear magic. Roan was thrown back, smashed into my collection of valuable comic books I hadn't sold yet, and fell to the floor motionless.

Alay aimed her clear magic staff and shot a blast at

the spinning red bubble that was still going around the shop. It hit my spell and dissipated the bubble immediately. Shelby and Corey fell to the floor and started puking on my carpet. Before anything was said and done, I nailed both Shelby and Corey with raw red energy. They never knew what hit them. They instantly became unconscious.

Topec and I stood shoulder to shoulder, ready to face Alay and her clear magic. Alay let out a bolt of clear magic. It came straight at me. Before I could duck, Topec pushed me out of the way and received the full brunt of the vicious attack. He flew backwards, hit a grandfather clock, and sagged to the floor. That left only my sister and me.

It was still pretty dark inside despite the door open. I willed the door back on the door hinges and closed. Now the shop was dark. Not pitch black, but dark.

"Where's the book, Arcadis? Tell me and I'll spare

your miserable life."

"Somehow I don't believe you. And my life's not so miserable. I get out, enjoy going to the movies, going to a museum now and then and killing my sister, you know fun stuff."

"Always the jokester. When I am done with you there won't be anything left of you to joke about. Now, for the last time, where is the book of spells?"

I saw her move in front of me. She was maybe ten feet from my position.

"Sorry, but it's not here. Jackson, who devised the resistance, got here before you and stole it."

"Liar!" She let out a bolt of energy from her staff. I didn't want to leave anything to chance and ducked. The clear energy struck the wall and blew it apart. I mean ripped it to shreds. Light filtered in and I could see her clearly. She saw me too and did a double take.

"What happened to you? Why are you so red?"

"I was telling you the truth, Alay. Jackson did come and steal the book. I and a few other people came to reclaim it. There was a struggle which left me and Jackson having a tug of war with the book. I won."

"So, where is it?" she demanded as she raised her staff.

"Are you that daft, Alay?"

"What are you babbling about?"

"Once I took possession of the book, all the knowledge seared into my brain. The book crumpled and turned to dust. The book gave me unparalleled power, even infused me with yellow and blue magic. The whole process turned my skin, hair, and eyes red. I would've suggested you speak to one of the people here for confirmation, but since they're out cold, that won't work."

She lowered her staff. "How is that possible? I had the book, Mother had the book, and you said Jackson had it. Why did it prefer you?"

"You mean you knew that would happen?" I asked with surprise.

"Of course. New material is added daily, sometimes mere moments later. It was several weeks ago I had noticed a new piece explaining how to acquire the knowledge of the book to dramatically increase your power. It was weird because the story just appeared but it was dated from the 1600's. Anyway, I read it twice, tried what it said to do but nothing happened. By then it was time to implement my plan and take over the Convocation. I hid the book here hoping to retrieve it later and try again. And here you stand, having thwarted my plans yet again!"

"Alay, I didn't mean it to happen. All I wanted was the book to go back to its original owner, our mother. I didn't ask for this power. I didn't choose it, it chose me."

Alay was lost in thought. "So that's what the book

meant."

"What are you talking about?"

She refocused. "In one passage it said, 'Don't ask for the power and it shall come to you.' I wanted it so badly but after reading the story, I realized I was doing the exact opposite of what it said. That's why I hid the book here. I figured if I left the book here, the book would think I didn't ask for it, you did since it was at your place. I wanted to come back here to let the book think you wanted the power for yourself and not me."

"Do you know how crazy that sounds to me? I think you, Jackson, and our mother wanted the power and the book knew that. I didn't want it and didn't ask for it. Hell, I didn't even know anything about the book."

Alay raised her staff. There was a tear in her eye. "I really didn't want it to end this way. When I learned of your existence, I had hoped to become friends." She wiped away the tear but never took her eyes off me.

"You know, do brother and sister stuff together."

"We still could, Alay. Just put down the staff and we can talk," I implored.

She laughed. "You look so weird with red hair." Then she grew more serious. "No, you want the staff for yourself. It would complete the cycle."

"Complete the cycle? Why do I feel you know a great deal more than I do?"

"You know, the cycle! You were born a primary, inherited Lord Quill's power, absorbed the book, you now have the three primary powers within you, I can sense it. With the clear magic, it would complete the process."

I became exasperated. "What process, Alay?"

"The process of completely ruling all of the realms. It's in the book. There's just one problem."

I sighed. "I don't want to take over the realms, but humor me. What's the problem?"

"The Wizard king, Anala knows about the book. He

has unbelievable power, comparable to yours, and has the clear magic staff. He seeks to overthrow the Warlocks to get the other staff. He'll overthrow them first because they're not of much as a threat since they're smaller in numbers and not as powerful. Then once he has both clear magic staffs he'll come after us."

"How do you know all of this?"

"It's in the prophecy section of the book, dumbass. Haven't you been listening to anything I have said?"

"Sure I have but I like listening to your storytelling skills. They're really good."

Alay shifted her foot, and aimed the staff in my direction. "Goodbye, Brother."

I instantly raised a three foot shield all around me. The blast came charging and it penetrated my shield. I extended the shield for a reason. The clear energy dispersed mine. As it came closer I could discern where the displacement occurred. I moved out of harm's way.

I repeated it again and again as the blasts continued.

I was hoping to stall her until someone woke up. Was the clear power that much more powerful? I heard someone stir awake. Finally! My mood rose until I noticed it was Shelby and not one of my troops. For Lord Quill's sake, will anything ever go my way just once? I didn't mind slugging it out with both of them if Alay didn't possess that damned staff. I decided to take the easy way out. When Shelby rose, it gave me a second reprieve. I hit Shelby with a quick blast and sent her reeling into Alay. Both fell. Alay got up but Shelby didn't. Wow, ya gotta love my newfound power. My quick blast equaled my old powerful blast. Alay shook her head.

"You are much more powerful, Arcadis, I'll give you that much, but it won't help you. You can keep avoiding my blasts, but sooner or later one will strike you!"

She was right. On the other hand, I had been playing defensive magic. It was time I started leveling the field and played offensive. Instead of waiting for her to strike, I threw the first punch, metaphorically speaking. I conjured up a spell and thrust it at her. She saw my pentagram turn red, so she expected it. What she didn't realize was I knew she was going to expect it. A split second later after my initial blast, I used my eye beams and scored a direct hit in her stomach. She doubled over and the staff fell to the floor near her. She went to pick it up but my mother snatched it before Alay could get her hands on it. Was my mother playing possum?

"I have had enough of you, young lady," My mother said as she raised the staff to her own flesh and blood.

"What are you doing, Mother?" I yelled.

"I can't let her transgressions go, Arcadis. She needs to be dealt with, permanently!"

"You can't do that! She is your daughter, for Lord Quill's sake!"

My mother's small frame stiffened. Her bony hand

held a firm grip on the staff. "Are you questioning my decision, Arcadis?"

Hell, I was in trouble with her before, I might as well be in trouble again. "Yes!"

My mother backtracked from Alay but never wavered. She came close to me. "You dare to judge me? Do you think your enhanced power gives you the right to supersede my decision?"

She was mad. I haven't seen her that mad since the spell Alay had cast on her infusing her will with magic.

"No, of course not, Mother. I don't want to see her die. I would like, with your permission, to take her and have her reconditioned with no red tape, excuse the pun. She was in prison for a while and never received any treatment."

"You would spare her life even though she sought to annihilate yours?"

I locked eyes with Alay. I saw a sister I never had.

I wanted to get to know her, hang out with her, watch her get married and the other things brothers and sisters were suppose to do.

"Yes. I'm begging you, Mother. I will not try to stop you if you chose to end her life. I will abide by your rules. You are the Convocation and I respect the institution. All I'm asking is to show leniency." She softened her stance. I tried again. "Please, Mother. No more killings, at least for today."

Slowly my mother lowered the staff. I quickly put a bubble around Alay lest she get any stupid ideas. She tried to break through the enclosure but my magic was much more powerful than hers.

My mother turned to me. I saw tears streaming down her face. "I almost killed my little girl. I don't know what got into me. If you hadn't been here, I would have killed her."

She allowed me to hug her while she cried. After a

moment, she regained her composure. She stood up, stared at Alay then turned to me. "Bring her to the re-conditioning room immediately. I will approve it."

I bowed, then walked to the bubble, created another one that encompassed me and the other bubble and, willed myself to the prison section of the hospital.

CHAPTER SEVEN

The reconditioning part of the hospital spooked me. There were several dozen rooms lined up on each side of the corridor. Each tiny room that housed only a desk, chair, and a monitor. Nothing else. The walls were white as was the carpet. Nothing to divert the attention of the occupant. I only knew that because I had put other people in here before. The beauty of the reconditioning process was it was only a onetime event. The whole process usually took ten and a half hours. But I didn't mind waiting.

I had the official document my mother signed and handed it to the woman at the front desk. Her bored expression told me she had done this job for way too long. She was pleasant looking, albeit on the chunky side. She wore a green uniform which was indicative of her power.

Her hair was brown, long, and parted on the side. She had the thickest coke rimmed glasses I have ever seen in my life. She was chewing gum. Loudly. I saw on her name tag. Denise. Denise, for her part, was staring at my hair and eyes. I will have to get used to that.

"Follow me, please."

I nudged Alay forward. She had a red prison uniform on and I had to put the magical bracelets back on to negate her power. For good measure, I put another pair on her ankles. We hadn't talked at all. I guess she was resigned to her fate. But really, it was better this way. When she came out of the recondition room she would be a new person. At least, that's what I hoped. We walked to the first room on the right. Denise extracted a thick set of keys from her side pocket and unlocked the door. I sat Alay down on the chair. She looked up at me.

"Please don't do this to me, Arcadis. I'll do whatever you say, whatever you want!"

I shook my head. "You had your chance and you fumbled on more than one occasion." I addressed Denise. "Proceed." I watched as Denise strapped Alay in the chair. I noticed the chair and desk were bolted so the patient couldn't move. Denise took magical tape and taped Alay's eyes open. She opened the desk drawer and took out electrodes. She plugged one end into the monitor and removed a protective film off the other end and affixed it to Alay's head in eight different places. Then she went back into the drawer and took out a pair of earphones and placed them over Alay's ears. She tapped some keys on the keyboard and opened a program. "Which selection, Mr. Gildeon?"

"Beg your pardon?"

She pointed to the screen. There were literally hundreds and hundreds of files in alphabetical order. I scanned some of them. Air traffic controller, beautician, doctor, lawyer, and a myriad of other professions. What a novel concept. I scrolled to the S's. I was hoping for something to do with sisterhood. There wasn't anything resembling it.

"I don't see what I would like her to do or be."

Denise leaned over my shoulder and her breasts wedged against my back. "What were you thinking?"

"I want her to be a normal sister and have a profession."

She stood up and slapped me on the back. "Why didn't you say so? That's a different folder, silly." A few minutes ago she was a bored woman, now she seemed to have become jovial.

She stroked more keys and another directory came up. She scrolled down, found what she was looking for and opened it. A long list populated on the page. All the folders started with Sister and... I went down the list searching for something specific. I finally found it near the end. Sister and Warrior. The W was at the end of the list. Duh. I pointed to the folder I selected. Denise looked at it and nodded. She opened the file. She had to give her initials to advance to the next page. I saw a small timer in the upper right hand corner. Twenty four hours and forty three minutes.

"I thought reconditioning was only ten and a half hours, Denise."

She pressed her hips against mine. "That's for one program like a photographer, auto mechanic, nurse, et cetera. You want two programs in one. I presume you want her to behave like she was your sister and be a warrior too?"

"She *is* my sister. I want her to act like my sister. Long story. I need her to be a warrior because there's a war still being fought out there and they're may be another biggie on the horizon."

"Okay, but you still want two programs at one time. Reconditioning is a very specific and exact science.

We've been doing this for over two hundred years."

I folded my arms. "Really? And what is your success rate?"

She started grinding her hips into mine. I moved away. She really needed to get out more often. "We boast a ninety nine point nine percent rate."

"What happened to the point one percent?"

"Oh, every once in a great while... maybe once every thirty-seven years, give or take a decade, someone dies while viewing a program."

"When was the last time someone died watching one of these programs?" I inquired.

"About fifteen years ago."

"I can handle the odds," I remarked.

"You can, what about me?" thundered Alay.

"Alay, you're too mean to become the point one percent. I have the utmost confidence in you." I leaned toward the monitor and noticed the screen was separated into two different videos for a lack of a better term. "Why is the screen divide like that, Denise?" I made sure I moved out of her way before she leaned down.

She emitted an audible sigh. "There are two programs on the screen because you chose two categories. The one on the left will go to her left temporal lobe and her left ear. The other program will go to her right temporal lobe and her right ear. It's almost akin to entrainment. Have you ever heard of it?"

"No, and I don't have the time for an explanation. Perhaps when the war is done and there's more time for frivolous endeavors, I may choose to."

"You're sexy when you're sarcastic. Let's just say the brain can handle it and both occupations will merge to-gether to produce one complete livelihood."

"Fine. Now, suppose she had to go to the bathroom or she gets hungry. Do you stop the programs?"

She became indignant. "Absolutely not! Then we

would have to start over and the success rate plummets. We've tried that before, Mr. Gildeon."

"Then what happens?"

"Then she gets hungry, expels piss, and expunges feces in her pants. It has to be that way or you might as well take her out of the reconditioning unit right now. I mean it."

I held up my hands in submission. "Okay, Denise you win. I have to go now. Alay, I will be back for you in twenty five hours. I'm giving you extra time in case there's any mess to be cleaned up."

"Thanks for nothing, Brother. For your sake, it had better work or I'm coming after you!"

"Ouch," Denise said.

"I know, right? Sisters these days." I saw Denise turn on the programs and the screen started. Denise left and I followed her out and closed the door. She took out her keys and locked the door. Before she could say anything else inappropriate, I practically ran through the doors and headed for the infirmary.

The infirmary wasn't far from the reconditioning unit. I was looking forward to see Ciana. When I got there, I headed to the nurses' station. A tall, green powered nurse was doing paperwork. Glancing around, I saw a lot of the beds were unoccupied. It was a good sign.

"Excuse me. May I speak to Ciana?"

She didn't look up. "She's with a patient in one of the treatment rooms in the back hallway. No one's allowed in there."

"When will she return?" I inquired nicely.

"Don't know, don't care."

"Well, I care. I'll ask you nicely one more time. When will she return?"

"Listen Buster..." She glanced up and did a double take. I guess the red hair, eyes, and a tinged red skin would do that.

"Oh, I'm sorry, Mister Gildeon! We have all sorts of nut jobs coming in... no offense! I didn't mean you, Sir. Please don't kill me!"

I chuckled. She amused me. I read her badge. "Lucy. I would really like to see Ciana. Now, please."

"Of course, Sir!" She reached for the phone and dialed. A few seconds passed. "That's odd. There's no answer."

I leaned toward her. "Would you care if I took it upon myself to go back there and find her?"

"No... no, Sir. Please feel free."

I thanked her and headed for the back hallway. I saw the long corridor with rooms on both sides but I forgot to ask Lucy what room Ciana was in. I willed up my red magic and pushed it forward. The red mist soon engulfed the entire hallway. I was looking for her signature wavelength. I found it, last door on the right.

I didn't sense anyone else except Ciana and her patient. Odd to have so many rooms and not utilize them. I came to the door and tried it. It was locked. I knocked. No one answered. I knocked again.

"We're busy! Get the hell out of here, this is a restricted area!" It was a male voice. I decided to be a jerk and knocked again. After a few more seconds, I knocked again. I heard the guy curse as he came barreling toward the door. He swung open the door while yelling, "What are you deaf..." then saw me. I saw him. He was barely dressed. "...Damn!" said the stranger. I walked in and saw Ciana was barely dressed too.

"So, this is the treatment you were telling me about." I said to Ciana while the guy was hurriedly dressing himself.

"Woman, you didn't tell me you knew the son of Lord Quill!"

"Hey, there'll be none of that," I said as I gave him a slight magical push. He flew into the wall and fell down.

The outline of his backside was embedded in the drywall. That had to hurt.

"Put your clothes on, Ciana." I used a floating spell and her clothes came to her in midair.

The stranger got dressed and ran out the door.

"It's not what you think, Arcadis."

I folded my arms in stubbornness. "Really? These treatment rooms aren't a bordello?"

She ran to me and slapped me in the face. "How dare you call me a prostitute!"

"If the magical shoe fits..."

She finished getting dressed and stormed out. I followed her but she wouldn't slow down. I weighed my options. If she made it to the infirmary, I wouldn't be able to talk to her. I put a red wall in front of her. She tried and couldn't get through it. She used her formable blue magic but the wall still stood. She stood there, motionless. I heard her take a few deep breaths before she turned around.

"Do you always have to use magic to get your way? The all-powerful son of Lord Quill! Hey everyone, if I don't get my way, I'll fry you!"

I came to her. "You know that's not true. I could have kicked the door down. I could have let that idiot disrespect you. I could have not let him go and pulverized him, but I didn't do any of those things."

She was livid. Her blue eyes bugged out. "How magnanimous of you, Arcadis."

"You misconstrue my intention, Ciana."

She came within inches of my face. She was almost as pretty as Surla, the Chronicler. "What exactly is your intention?"

"I came here to discuss a war."

"I know about the war, everyone does! There are still scattered pockets of resistance from the rebellious secondaries. Now, please remove the wall so I can resume work."

"You seemed to be working on him."

"Jealous, Arcadis? How unbecoming of you."

"I will let you go under two conditions."

"You're not going to lower the wall until I listen to your prattle?"

"That is correct."

She threw up her hands in exasperation. "So be it."

"The first one is about the war."

"I know about the war!"

"Will you stifle it? I am not talking about the current war! I am talking about the war that is currently brewing between our magical race, the Wizards, and the Warlocks."

"How would you know?" Then recognition came upon her face. "The book?"

"Yes."

She looked confused. "What can I do about it? I'm

no warrior."

"True, but there is an ancient law I know about that states the Convocation are allowed to call upon the populace in times of war."

She held up her hand to stop me. "If it's ancient, it pertains to Lord Quill. He didn't exactly see eye to eye with my gender."

"Forgive me if I'm wrong, but didn't my mother engage in battle?"

When I invoked my mother's name, Ciana's ears perked up. "Yes, but she is the most powerful sorcerer there is, except for you."

"She's still a female. She didn't abide by Lord Quill's rule."

"Why are you telling me this?"

"I intend to hold a meeting with the Convocation. I want every available colored powered being to be reconditioned to be a warrior."

She was flabbergasted. "Are you out of your mind?"

"Possibly. But if we are at war with other magical beings, what chance do we have of winning if we don't have the necessary troops?"

"But I am a nurse. I will be needed here!"

"You'll be needed on the battlefield. They have re-conditioning programs that allow dual professions. I should know, my sister is currently there."

"You want me to be a nurse and a warrior? Forget it mister! There is no way in hell I am going to do that."

"If the Convocation decrees it you will. Remember I am now a Regulator. I will make damn sure you abide by their ruling."

She looked me up and down. "That book has changed you, Arcadis."

"Be that as it may, I am going to the Convocation after we finish here."

"Suppose they say no to your ingenious plan?"

"I can be very persuasive. I have no intention of taking no for an answer."

"I think your newfound power has gone to your head."

"On the contrary. I now have more clarity than ever."

"Okay, skip to your second condition. I'm done talking to you about your insane plan."

I smiled. She had no qualms about expressing what she thought. "The second condition is explaining to me what you were doing in the treatment room with Mr. Happy Go Lucky."

Ciana frowned. She seemed hesitant. "I don't really want to discuss that with you, Arcadis. It's above your pay grade."

"Now you piqued my curiosity."

"I am not allowed to discuss it with you."

"I could probe you."

"You wouldn't dare!"

"Try me."

"NO!"

"Why not? Is it nurse patient confidentiality?"

She remained silent. I let the minutes slip by. The first five minutes she brooded. The next ten minutes she was steaming. By twenty minutes she got up and banged on my red wall. Her fists were pulsating primary blue energy.

"Arcadis! Let me out!"

I remained defiant. "No, not until you tell me what's going on."

"You are one stubborn bastard."

"I've been accused of that before. I'm okay with it. Please tell me what's going on, Ciana. I'm sure you're needed in the infirmary by now."

She sat down. "Damn you, Arcadis."

I sat down beside her and gave her a nudge. "That's the spirit!"

She removed her hat and ran her hand through her

black hair. "If I tell you, will you promise to keep your mouth shut?"

"Of course." I said as I crossed my heart.

"Remember, this is still part of the Convocation and you're sworn to abide by your word."

"I know."

"Okay, here goes everything. We were just about to get hooked up to a machine. The device collects sperm from the male and eggs from a female."

I was floored. "Why? Wouldn't you want to do it the old fashioned way to get pregnant? And why would you want a baby with that guy? He was a jerk."

"Oh boy, am I going to get into trouble. We have a huge research and development facility offsite. For the last thirty years, since Lord Quill's death, we have been actively trying to repopulate the primaries. At first we did copulate but that took too long."

"I don't like where this is headed, Ciana."

"You're the stubborn idiot who wouldn't leave things alone. About five years ago, we achieved a medical breakthrough. We were able to accelerate the process to a point where we could produce a primary colored being within three months versus nine months."

"What about the developmental aspects? A baby needs parents, a loving home, and time to grow up."

"The breakthrough allowed the fetus to grow at an accelerated rate. By the time three months had elapsed, the child was fully grown. We immediately place him or her in the reconditioning unit. It was no accident the reconditioning unit was placed not far from here. "

"You chose what occupation the children were going to do with their lives?"

She shrugged her shoulders. "It's no different than you placing your sister in there."

"Then why are you so adamant about my plan to put everyone in the reconditioning unit?"

"Because you're only supposed to recondition someone once in their life. If you happened to put one of the primaries we grew into a reconditioning unit that already had been in one, it could prove disastrous."

I sighed. "You really know how to deflate someone. Your admission puts me in a quandary."

"Maybe it was for the best I told you. Your mother is bound to reject your idea."

"I figured my mother had a hand in this."

"Nothing is done without the Convocation's approval."

I thought for a second when a sudden realization hit me. Actually two realizations.

"Why would you need to be nude with that guy? If you were having your eggs removed, you wouldn't need him in the room to do it. And vice versa."

"I had to be nude with him to see if his sperm and my eggs were compatible. The device was decoding my egg's DNA and his sperm genetic makeup to make sure there were no abnormalities when you knocked. We have to make sure the strongest sperm is extracted and I have to have viable eggs. There were tests we needed to do together."

Make that three realizations. She just answered one of them. "How did you two hook up? An online dating service that catered to fertile sorcerers?"

She smirked. "No, ignorant one. It's a voluntary group. Word of mouth is the best form of advertising. And by the way, happens to be one of the best magical surgeons we have."

Two down, one to go. "If I understand what is going on then some of these primaries walking around are actually your children, am I correct?"

"Yes."

"How does that make you feel?"

Ciana exhaled air. "The cause justifies the means. I do

feel maternal pangs and motherly but we aren't allowed to associate with them. Don't think for one second I am the only one doing this either, Arcadis. But, once my eggs are removed I am removed from the picture."

"Do you ever walk down a street, go into a store and look around at the people and think, 'Gee, that woman looks like me, I wonder if she was one of my eggs?'"

Sadness engulfed her. "Of course I do, or did. Not so much anymore. I can't think like that, Arcadis. It would drive me nuts."

I touched her knees and felt a tingling sensation. "I'm surprised they haven't asked me to donate my sperm."

"I'm sure there'll come a time when it will come to that."

I had an idea. "Why don't the people being currently hatched be reconditioned to become a warrior?"

"They're not hatched. They're sorcerers like you and me, numb nuts. I don't want the up and coming generation becoming militarized. It sounds like we'd become a police state."

"But that's what the Regulators are."

"There are a lot fewer Regulators than sorcerers being born every day. Besides, some of the people do become warriors. Not much percentage wise. As a matter of fact, you will have new Regulator recruits in the next few days."

"Will they be primary or secondary?"

"Primary, why?"

"It won't work. The Regulators are proud driven secondary powers that go back to Lord Quill's era."

"They'll get used to it."

"Seriously, Ciana? You think there's a class war now? Take away their livelihood, their reason for being and you will have the fight of your life on your hands. If you ask any secondary power what their ultimate goal was, invariably all of them would say they wanted to become a Regulator. They're fiercely loyal and that's why the Convocation likes having them as protectors."

"But we can instill that attribute into the primaries through reconditioning."

"There's a big difference between genuine loyalty and loyalty that was placed in their psyche, Ciana."

She stood and pointed to the red wall. "I'm done discussing semantics with you, Arcadis. Please remove the wall." I sighed, got up and willed the wall away. "Thank you, Jerk."

When the red wall lowered, Ciana hurried through the door, ignoring the throng of people lingering about. Sure, I probably embarrassed her but I did manage to glean useful information. My next step was to determine what to do with the information. I wasn't allowed to speak to my mother about the accelerated sorcerer birth process. Then how was I to build up an army with an impending war we could ill afford? I walked through the infirmary, ignoring the looks of the nurses' and doctors'. They probably saw the expression on Ciana's face as she slammed through the door. I was headed through the corridor which led to my mother's office. The desks were all repaired, even the secondary ones. Similarly, all of the colored powered doors were fixed after Lucinda and her shadowlins attacked some time ago.

As I walked amongst the magical repair crews, I saw Topec, Roan, and Aredous walking hurriedly and with purpose towards me. Their posture was stiff. Topec's brown eyes bored into my red eyes when I noticed an interesting change in his, and the other two, appearances. All three of them had their respective colored trench coats buttoned up. I had never seen any of the Regulators button up their coats. I noticed they were flanked, effectively blocking my path.

Here we go again. What did I do this time? Topec raised his arm and on some primal instinctual level the flight or fight mode kicked in. I raised a red shield all around me lest I get attacked by all three of them. Instead of Topec's gold sword suddenly appearing out of nowhere, because I've seen him do it, he held an envelope and handed it to me. I lowered my shield and raised an eyebrow. I warily accepted it. I turned it around to study. It was sealed with the Convocation's emblem which was a triangle that had a space where the lines were supposed to meet. All three lines were brown which were the three primary colors merged. Where there was space where the lines were supposed to meet, there was a straight line coming out of all three sides, and each line that came out had the red, blue, and yellow colors. The envelope itself had the primary colors evenly divided on the back and front.

I turned it over again. "What's this? Another summons?" All three of the Regulators shifted uncomfortably.

"Yes and no." Topec was apparently the spokesperson for the group. His deep voice was neutral which made it hard for me to discern the level of trouble I was in.

"I thought a solicitor had to issue one of these nasty official looking papers." I flapped the envelope like a fan. "And why are the three of you here with your trench coats buttoned up?"

"Arcadis, for the love of Lord Quill! Shut up and open the envelope already!" Topec thundered. His voice resonated across the wide expanse of the lobby. Heads turned but I ignored them.

I hesitantly opened the envelope, extracted the paper, and saw it was folded in threes. I unfurled it and read. It only took several seconds. "Guys, this letter is vague. I have to meet the Convocation tomorrow at ten a.m.? What's this about?"

Roan piqued up. "Sorry Arcadis, you know the rules. We're not allowed to tell you."

"But, I have to get my sister out of Reconditioning tomorrow. Can't we postpone whatever nonsense I'll be subjected to?"

"Not everything the Convocation does is nonsense, Arcadis. I take offense to that," Ardeous intoned.

I bowed. "My apologies, Ardeous. I am very frustrated. Please let the Convocation know I will be there."

"Why are you being so nice about this, Arcadis?" Roan asked with mild surprise.

I looked them over. "It's not every day the three most senior Regulators give you a notice to appear before the Convocation. Now, would you mind stepping aside?"

"Why, where are you going?" Topec asked.

"Why do you want to know? Are you interested or is the Convocation?"

"Arcadis, I must be candid with you. Since the battle with Lucinda, you've gone through a metamorphosis no sorcerer has ever gone through. We are looking out for our self interest as a society. We don't know if you're a savior or a walking time bomb and that scares us. We don't like being scared."

"Is it the red hair? My red eyes? The red tinged skin?"

"It's much more than that, idiot! The all-powerful Lord Quill's magic radiates through you. You were able to absorb the most potent book of spells that was ever created. That book is pure magic. I was told even the wizards know about the books existence. Do you know how really powerful you've become? What do you think?"

"Topec, I think you and everyone else are being paranoid. True, I have been through some rough spots lately, but I am handling them just fine. *Now, back off and let me pass.*"

Topec, Roan, and Ardeous stepped aside, each watching me as I walked past them.

By now I was too mad to speak to my mother and

wanted nothing to do with the conflict. I would help the Regulators tomorrow. I didn't think a night off would make a difference. As I walked down the corridor and turned right toward my room, I had a sudden revelation. Topec and the other Regulators apparently don't trust me, I wonder if the Convocation did. It would make sense for them to have someone follow me in case I did flip out. It would have to be someone clever in the arts because I can usually tell if I am being trailed. I turned around to see if I were being paranoid. I didn't see anyone but if Alay could do it, I wondered if there were anyone else that was secretly trained that could.

I got to my room, found pajamas with the justice league characters, and put them on. It always amused me that superheroes in the comics weren't real but sorcerers, wizards, and warlocks were. I went to bed discouraged because I no longer knew my place in the sorcerer's world. It's not like I knew my place but I was getting to the point of feeling comfortable, then I gained the entire contents of the book of knowledge and now I'm back to square one. And I was nervous concerning tomorrow's meeting, but hopeful I would get my sister back. I was missing my simpler life in McCordsville with my antique shop. Don't get me wrong, I loved the augmented power, but now I had much more responsibility. I fell asleep and the last thought in my mind was Topec wearing that awful aftershave.

CHAPTER EIGHT

I had set my internal alarm clock to go off at eight-thirty. When the internal alarm rang, I immediately got up, showered, and dressed. I needed red powered coffee in the worst way.

At the cafeteria I sat alone in my thoughts. People walked by and bowed but no one came and sat next to me. I wondered if anyone sat with any of the senior members of the Convocation.

I hung around until nine-thirty and couldn't take it any longer. I took the long way to the assembly room where I was supposed to meet with the Convocation. By the time I reached the door and opened it, it was quarter to ten.

I sat at the table I had sat at when I was on trial. I brushed off some lint I saw on my red trench coat. Finally, people started trickling in. Soon the room was filled, but the ambiance was different. Today no one wanted to kill me or see me dead.

My mother, Arrake, and Garnom came in and everyone got up. We waited until they were seated before we sat. Thankfully they didn't have their silly colored wigs on. The solicitor was here but he was merely a spectator. My mother struck her red gavel, Arrake struck his blue gavel next, then Garnom struck his yellow gavel. Interesting, that had never occurred before. I was filled with dread as a hush filled the assembly room.

"Arcadis Ander Gildeon, please rise," my mother shouted. I complied. All eyes were focused on me. "Son, as you are aware, one of your new duties is being a Regulator. This is the official ceremony. You will be sworn in by the three of the senior members of the Convocation. Are you ready?"

I bit my lip because I didn't want any of the unnecessary attention. So this was what the summons was for? Had I known, I would have skipped this part! "Yes I am." I replied calmly which belied my true feelings. I placed my right hand over my pentagram.

"Arcadis, do you swear to uphold the fundamental laws of the sorcerer's whether or not they coincide with your beliefs, dogmas, or philosophical slant?"

That one would be a toughie. "Yes, I swear I will."

"Do you swear allegiance to protect the senior members and regular members of the Convocation?"

That one was easy. "Yes, I do so swear."

"And do you Arcadis, swear not to divulge any secret that is shared with you, so help you Lord Quill?"

That one would be hard. I was dying to talk to my mother concerning what I learned from Ciana. "Yes, I so swear."

"Then by the order of the Convocation, you are now officially the head of the Regulators, congratulations,

Son!" She stood up and clapped. Everyone followed. Then one by one each of the remaining Regulators came to me and shook my hand. I noticed all of their colored trench coats were buttoned up. Then I understood why Topec and the others had their coats buttoned up. They probably had an official meeting yesterday to nominate me before they came looking for me.

"Arcadis, come forward," my mother commanded. I obeyed and walked over to the huge desk. "Please remove your trench coat."

"My trench coat? But, I love this one." I said earnestly.

My mother smiled. "Don't worry, you'll get it back."

I took it off and the red instantly changed to black. She took hold of it and the other senior members held it too. They closed their eyes and the Convocation emblem etched itself onto the upper left corner of my jacket. I saw the three lines of the triangle slowly turn brown as the three primary powers infused their magic. The space where the lines were almost met that formed the triangle now had three lines coming out from the inside. Each line had one of the three primary colors. The middle of the triangle was brown but would probably change to the color of my power once the coat was placed on me.

"Arcadis, you are now officially in charge of the Regulators. Your new title will be Overseer."

I was stunned. I was in charge? But, I had no experience. A billion thoughts crossed my mind as I bowed.

"But Mother, I am a primary and they shouldn't be in charge of the Regulators." I said that in hopes of opening up a discussion concerning primaries being bred for Regulator duties. Judging by my mother's reaction, she did not correlate the two. If she did, she was a great actor.

My mother looked at the Regulators in the room. "Yesterday's meeting was about that very topic, Son. There was a vote and it was unanimous. Now, if that weren't good news enough, here's more." My mother nodded to someone several feet behind her. He left and returned a second later with Alay! Alay came rushing toward me with outstretched arms. I hurried around the table and met her. We hugged for several seconds. "Arcadis, you look fantastic! Wow! Look at your hair, eyes, and skin! The picture I saw you in, you didn't look like that!" she said smiling.

I was bewildered. "What are you talking about, Alay? I have seen you plenty of times in the past several days."

Her face shifted a little. She turned to our mother. "What's he talking about, Mother? You told me we had never met."

My mother looked at me with her stern eyes. "Pay no heed to him, Alay. With all the fanfare concerning his promotion, the continued resistance, and the book of spells engulfing him, he is probably confused. Isn't that right, Arcadis?"

Ah, got it. The reconditioning. It must have started her life from scratch. "Mother's right, Alay. There has been so much going on lately, I don't know what's going on!" I released her grip, went to the bench and retrieved my coat. When I put it on, the black turned to red. I looked at the emblem and the inside of the triangle did turn red. The etching made the symbol stick out which I thought was cool. I traced the outline a few times with one of my fingers, then looked at my mother and whispered, "My apologies, I forgot the reconditioning started at birth."

"All is well, Son. Now, you have a big day ahead of you. We found out where the resistance stronghold is and we are planning a major offensive in less than an hour. Are you up to it, Overseer?"

"Yes, yes I am."

"Good. Meet me in my office with Alay in five minutes."

I nodded and went back to Alay. "We have to meet

Mother in her office in five minutes. Are you ready to do some battle?"

Her sweet disposition changed when I uttered the word battle. Her mouth went from a smile to a sneer, her face wrinkled and she brought up a sword that pulsated red. "I am ready to do battle and with you by my side, I have no doubt we will win!"

Great, I hope she didn't preach when it came to actual battle. I walked toward the door, stopped and raised my voice. "Whoever is coming with me to fight follow me to my mother's office!"

I saw several dozen shades of colored power emanate from raised swords, staffs, and wands. They cried in unison, "All hail Arcadis, the Overseer!" They repeated it several times. I got a little emotional, something I hate to do. However, I felt I had to join in too. I raised my right arm and shot a red power bolt. Not too strong or I would have taken down the high ceiling. I left with Alay right behind me. The others joined as we marched to my mother's office.

"How many warriors do we have?" Alay asked as we walked the long corridor.

I inclined my head and faced her as we turned left. Out of my peripheral vision, I saw my mother's office down the hall. "You mean sorcerers, not warriors, right?"

She waved her hand in dismissal. "Yeah, yeah, that's what I meant."

As we continued to walk down the hallway, I wondered if I should be concerned with Alay's response. I looked down because I could not hear my feet on the red, blue, and yellow carpet, it was so thick. I was close to the tri-colored wall and reached out and touched it. It was fibrous and rubbery, which disgusted me. Finally we reached my mother's door to her office. I was about to knock when Surla came out. The Chronicler was dressed much more conservatively than normal. I was disappointed. She had a white blouse and black trousers, nothing fancy or enticing. She was with Topec and Roan. I thought they were celebrating with me, apparently not.

"What's up, guys?" I asked nonchalantly. They appeared serious and determined.

"We are on assignment by the order of the senior members of the Convocation," Surla responded way too seriously.

"Where are you headed?" I asked in a friendly voice.

Topec rushed up to me. His muscles were taut and his posture was stiff. "It's private, *Overseer*," he sneered as he emphasized the last word.

"Listen Topec, I've had just enough out of you..."

He came closer. "Really? And what are you going to do about it?"

Surla intervened. She seemed to do that a lot lately. "Topec, you will respect the Overseer. Arcadis, be pleasant. Now, shake hands or I will inform Madame Gildeon."

When Topec heard her name, he instantly backed away. "I am sorry... Arcadis. With the secondaries' battles and this clandestine operation, I got a little anxious."

I bowed and he returned the gesture. It must be a serious expedition for Topec to be so overtly worried.

They rushed past us as Alay and I entered our mother's office. It was packed with primaries and secondaries. People backed away and let us get to the front. My mother was discussing something with a group of people. She sensed our presence, looked up and smiled.

"Children!" She looked to us. "You don't know how nice it sounds to finally be able to say that!"

We bowed. "What's going on, Mother?" Alay asked as she peered down at papers that were on her humongous desk.

Our mother pointed her gaunt finger at a map lying

flat on her spacious desk. More people were filing in, making it harder to get breathing room.

"Let's take everyone to the assembly room, it has a lot more room," my mother said as she noticed she didn't have much elbow room.

Everyone let us through and followed us. There was a swarm of people with all sorts of colored trench coats. I've never seen so many primaries and secondaries together.

We walked back to the meeting room where we just were. The room soon became crowded. Usually I would mind being so cramped but the more people that joined our cause, the better. I was up in front with the senior members and Alay. My mother had another map and she pointed at it with a skinny finger. "Arcadis, I'm not very good at reading maps, where is this location?"

I peered down to take a look. The satellite imagery was phenomenal. It showed a corn field in McCordsville, not far from my shop. "Why is everything centered at McCordsville?"

"Wasn't that question raised earlier?" someone from the back of the crowd yelled out.

I looked around the huge throng of people but couldn't see who the sarcastic person was. "Yes, it was raised earlier, Smartass. The book of spells was placed there and people challenged me to duels there, but other than that, there's no reason why the last vestige of the resistance would be hiding there." I picked up the map and displayed it for everyone. I pointed to a small circle for every person to see. "What I can't fathom is why they would pick the woods behind my store... oh boy."

My mother was puzzled. "What is it, Arcadis?"

I let out a deep breath. "The soul trees. They can seek out other enchanted soul trees to find any answer to any question posed."

"But, you no longer have an enchantment there,

they're not sentient."

"Anyone can put up an enchantment around any perimeter. The trick would be to convince the soul trees."

"I seem to recall you were able to communicate with them," my mother added.

I nodded my head. "Only after threatening to incinerate them. What if the remaining members of the group were really desperate, put up an enchantment and asked the soul trees how to defeat us?"

"How long would it take for the soul trees to provide them an answer assuming they were able to awake them?" Alay asked with concern.

"When I asked them how to defeat Lucinda, originally they said six hours. I told them they had three. But Lucinda predated them. They had to ask around the earth and other realms for any soul trees which had encountered the Bianca family. With the book of spells being around longer than the Bianca family, I would say it could last several hours. But they have had several hours to ask the soul trees."

"Then there's no time to waste. We need to get back to your antique shop pronto," Alay commented.

I wanted a show of force to the people who had defied the Convocation. There was an ample number of sorcerers for the task. "Who is willing to come to McCordsville and finally put an end to the struggle?"

I heard a chorus of cheers. One lone person in the back of the room raised her hand. She wore an emerald trench coat and wore way too much makeup. It wasn't gothic, just poorly applied. The black eyeliner was too thick for her face. Her tiny lips were blood red and she had too much blush on. Her short wavy hair was brown in every place but her roots. They were blond. And she was really, really tall.

"Yes?" I inquired.

"Uh, hi, my name is Rosinda. I am a secondary as you

already surmised. I have a question for you, Overseer."

Everyone's eyes turned to me. "Yes, Rosinda, what is it?" I asked nicely.

She looked down to the floor, shuffled her feet and looked back up at me. "Are you planning on killing the rest of the secondaries out there? We heard what you did to Jackson and we don't want it happening to our brethren."

I could see everyone's eyes on me. The secondaries outnumbered us here and I really didn't want another blood bath. "No, I don't want any more bloodshed. And I apologize for vaporizing Jackson, but he went berserk on everyone."

"So when you catch him and the others, what are you planning on doing with him? Are they going to trial?" Rosinda asked again.

I pointed to my mother because she ran things around here. "That would be up to the Convocation. Mother, can you answer that for us?" I hated to put her on the spot but she was in charge, it was her call. My mother stood straighter. She recognized the significance of her response.

"Jackson was the sole person responsible for the uprising. Since he is gone, the others will be put into jail until they are reconditioned. We don't want any more deaths on our hands."

Rosinda bowed. Apparently my mother's answer was better than being jailed, going on trial and being killed.

With the tension gone, I bid everyone to stand back. "Raise your hands if you want to follow us into battle."

Out of a few hundred people, seventy-five or so raised their hands. I willed some magic, filled the area in front of me with red magic and made a huge bubble appear. I walked in and people started filing in. Hopefully, this would be the last battle we would have with our own kind forever. We went in and I willed the bubble to my antique shop.

Chapter Nine

We came out of the red bubble in front of my store and walked in because the front door was ajar. I looked around. It was in shambles. Besides the mess the place endured from the previous battles that took place here, vandalism was rampant. All of my valuable comic books were gone, the two couches (Who would want them?) and everything that wasn't bolted to the ground. I took a quick inventory of the upstairs but thankfully the remnants of my lab were still there and intact.

I lead the way to the back of the door which was closed. Before I touched the door handle, I willed some magic to see if any trickery awaited us on the other side, but sensed none. I opened the door and walked outside and saw forty or so people in a large circle that encompassed part of the soul trees. They had their heads up facing the sky with their eyes closed.

"Are they communicating with the trees, Arcadis?" Alay asked as she brought up her red sword.

"I... I think so. Perhaps we should interrupt their party." Alay didn't need any more convincing. She lifted her red sword and shot a bolt of red lighting. It hit someone squarely in his back and he toppled over. Other primaries and secondaries continued with the plan Alay had laid out. Attack and ask questions later. I took a more careful approach despite being the strongest sorcerer there.

I willed my augmented magic to the soul trees and sought the representative I had spoken to previously. I saw him and walked toward the trees and ignored the battle. None of the secondaries chose to do battle with me and I was okay with that. "Soul tree representative, what has happened here?"

"You seem different, Arcadis. You are overflowing with red magic, much more than our preceding encounter."

"Long story. The abridged version is I absorbed the book of spells and my magical power increased exponentially."

"Then the myth of completing the cycle is true?" The soul tree was reaching out of the bark as far as he could without actually leaving.

I rolled my eyes. "No, I am not going to rule all of the realms and whatever tall tales that accompany it." The soul tree receded back into the bark but moved from left to right. The grain of the enchanted wood moved with him. "The secondaries enchanted you to find a way to defeat the primaries and the Convocation?"

"That was the plan. It took some exertion from the group since they weren't the original owners of the property."

"I see. Were you able to provide them with an answer?" I asked innocuously.

"We gave them part of the answer since they gave us more time than you did."

He was alluding to the fact I cut their time in half seeking answers about a way to defeat the Bianca family. The fight seemed eons ago. "Really? I would like to know what information you gave them, soul tree representative."

"Sorry, Son of Lord Quill, we can't do that. It's strictly a private discourse between them and us because they created the enchantment, not you."

I turned around and watched the battle for a few seconds. The outcasts were being rounded up. I was happy to note only a few sorcerers were lying on the ground. It could have been much worse. I sensed the enchantment was flimsy at best. I closed my eyes and willed a considerable amount of magic to penetrate the secondaries' combined enchantment.

"What are you doing, Arcadis? You can't just create an enchantment over an enchantment!" The soul tree envoy yelled to me.

"Who said anything about creating one to go over the other one? I am busting through theirs and putting up my own so you are required to tell me."

I heard more complaining, but ignored them. Penetrating the secondaries enchantment was a little more difficult than I thought, but after a moment, I managed to. I then put mine back in place.

The ambiance of the delegate I spoke to changed. His movement slowed in the bark. He and the others shook violently for a few seconds then returned to normal.

"Arcadis, Son of Lord Quill, what a pleasant surprise. We weren't expecting you."

I was perplexed. "We just finished having a conversation. Don't you remember?"

"No, this is the first time since you left. We have been hearing good things about you."

"I thought when I left, the enchantment was gone."

"You are very powerful, Arcadis. Your enchantment stuck around. It was dissipating very slowly. We were losing sentience until you just showed up."

I crossed my arms around my chest. "If you were somewhat sentient, why don't you recall the group of secondaries creating an enchantment around you earlier?"

"If they did, when you created yours, it must have displaced theirs. You have to remember, you're the original owner of the property, your spell would automatically revert the enchantment back to you, losing all information in the process."

I folded my arms over my chest in annoyance. "Damned convenient if you ask me."

The emissary bowed as much as he could and I reluctantly returned it. The conversation was over and I had no other recourse but to ask a group of people who loathed me what they were seeking from the soul trees.

I left and joined the waning fight. I threw a few bolts of red magic. Once I joined the fray, the remaining secondaries put up their hands in surrender.

A Regulator named Daral from Kentucky came over to me and bowed deeply. His trench coat was, umm.. periwinkle? He was tall, thin, had a scraggly beard and wore a fedora.

"Overseer, Alay has the organizer."

I bowed. "Please bring him to me." Daral left and returned a second later with Alay and a prisoner. He was a replica of Jackson.

"Why do you look like Jackson?" I asked the man. He too wore a violet trench coat and wore the same kind of glasses and blue eyes.

"I am his identical twin brother. I heard you vaporized him in cold blood, you bastard!" He made a feeble attempt to escape Alay's clutches.

"Look, Jackson's twin, I have no quarrel with you or any other person who sought to go against us. I just think you went about it the wrong way."

That shut him up but it brought a stern gaze from my mother.

"Daral, you're to bring him and the others to the magic free jail. Make sure they all have magical bracelets on too," my mother commanded.

"Mother, can we get the fallen to the infirmary? Some of them don't look too healthy. They may need the healer scan," I asked with worry.

"Of course, Son. Daral, coordinate with the other Regulators."

Daral's tall frame bowed deeply and my mother returned the gesture. Personally, I was getting sick of the bowing, but the tradition went back to the Lord Quill era. He demanded everyone do it to him, but he rarely returned the favor.

I walked amongst the crowd as we entered the back of my shop. Before leaving I wanted to do two things. Firstly, I made a powerful enchantment for the soul trees so no one could ever take them over again and it would allow them sentience for eternity. Secondly, I sought out Rosinda. She clearly towered over almost everyone. I could see her blond roots from afar. I cast a spell to immobilize her. She froze in place and peered around frantically. I willed in her mind not to panic, it was me, and I wanted to talk to her alone. Since she wasn't powerful enough to respond, she stood there until everyone left except us.

I motioned for Alay to leave without me. Several magical elevators appeared and all of them left. It was just Rosinda and me. I let her go and she ran up to me, went to her knees, and started to cry.

"Please don't kill me, Arcadis! Please, I'll do anything you ask!"

"Rise, Rosinda!" I commanded. I might as well play the role. I was going to ask her for a favor, but I thought she might be resistant. Since she thought I was going to kill her, I could use that to my advantage.

"Rosinda, the conflict was brief but through the brevity, I saw you fight well, although reluctantly." I actually did not see her fight nor did I know if she fought reluctantly.

She rose but refused to meet my eyes. "Sorry Overseer, it's just, they're like family to me."

"Family or not, they sought to overthrow the Convocation and that is unacceptable."

"I know, Sir. What are you going to do with me?" She finally looked up at me and there was a bustle of tears flowing down her overabundance of makeup.

"I will make you a deal. I will forget your transgression against the Convocation if you do one simple thing for me." She started to remove her clothing. "No, not that!" I shouted. She seemed confused. While she did possess a nice figure, I wanted information.

"Jackson's twin, what is his name?" I thundered.

She put her shirt back on quickly and went down on her knees again. She was terrified of me. I don't like people being afraid of me except when it's called for. This was one of those times.

"His name is Daniel, Sire."

"Are you friends with him? Do you know of him?"

"We dated a few times, nothing serious." She sounded remorseful.

"Would he speak with you if I allowed it?"

"Probably."

"Rosinda, that was a yes or no question." I glared at her when she looked up. She immediately put her head down.

"Yes, Overseer, yes I promise he will even if I have to make him!"

"Okay. We will go to the magical jail and you will ask him one question I have for him."

"Of course. Of course. What is the question, Overseer?"

"He had alone time with the soul trees in my backyard. They don't remember the conversation because I broke their enchantment and placed mine back. I need to know what he learned from the soul trees. Can you do that for me?"

She bowed. "Of course. I can be very persuasive with Daniel."

"Good, let's go. Time is of the essence."

I hastily conjured a red bubble, encased us, and left for the Convocation.

When we appeared, I made sure we were in the hallway where we were before we left. The jail was a several minute walk. Rosinda seemed cognizant I didn't trust her. Whether it hurt her feelings or not, I did not care. I had to know what the soul trees told Daniel. That was my priority.

We walked in silence. Everyone we met bowed to us. The trip was uneventful. When we arrived, the security guard let us through without incident. I was still curious as to how Mack got hold of Lord Quill's clear magic staff and how he even knew it existed. But that was for another day.

We were at the gate where Rosinda was to walk through and speak to Daniel. I stopped her before she entered. "Remember Rosinda, find out what I need and don't even think about betraying me." For emphasis I made sure red magic crackled from my fingertips.

Fear spread across her face. She regained her composure and nodded. I saw her enter through the one way window. She sat down tentatively and waited for Daniel to appear.

Daniel arrived a couple of minutes later. He seemed surprised she was there.

I looked around and found a switch so I could listen in on their conversation.

"What are you doing here, Rosinda? You have some gall coming here! You were supposed to help with our cause, not fight alongside them."

She tensed up. "Daniel, I am far more afraid of Arcadis and the Convocation than I am of you and your supporters."

Daniel pushed his glasses up. His umm... periwinkle prison outfit looked out of place. Then I noticed a person at a similar table at the back of the room. His prison uniform was pink. How was that possible? You would have to mix a red primary power with a white colored power but there was no such thing. I hailed the guard and he practically ran over to me.

"Yes, Overseer?" He seemed eager to please unlike his predecessor.

I pointed to the guy in the pink outfit. "How is that person a pink power? There are no white magical beings to mate with a red primary to produce that color."

"Begging your liege, but there are white powered people."

"Please explain." I crossed my arms.

"White powered people are normal citizens of earth. Caucasians, African Americans, Asian, Hispanic, Etc cetera. They have no power. We call them white power."

"But it's illegal to mate with a normal human."

He pointed to the inmate. "Hence that's why he is here. And his parents have to live the rest of their lives here at the Convocation so the humans don't find out about us."

I thanked him and he left. I looked to Rosinda and

their conversation was getting heated.

"I don't have to tell you anything and I don't owe you anything, Rosinda. Just get the hell out of here!" Daniel got up and called for the guard. The guard looked at me and I shook my head no. If Rosinda couldn't extract anything out of him, I would do it.

Rosinda ran through the door, saw me and burst out crying.

"I'm so sorry Sire, he wouldn't tell me anything. Please don't kill me!" She became frantic.

I held her tight. "Don't worry, Rosinda. You tried your best. Now, it's my turn." I brushed her aside.

"Please don't hurt Daniel, Sire. Please."

I motioned for the guard to get her out of my sight.

I walked into the large room on the magical side and a hush descended. There were a total of ten rows of tables with one seat on both sides. Three of them were occupied. When they saw me, they motioned the guards to let them back in their cell. Daniel saw me and banged on the door to get back into his cell but no one opened the door for him.

I walked closer and stopped in front of the table where he had sat. I sat down and patiently waited. After a few more futile attempts of banging frantically on the door, he finally gave up. He walked to table and reluctantly sat down. He looked at me and without warning, threw himself against the magical force field. He fell backwards, got up and sat back down. I didn't flinch.

"You're so tough on that side, Son of Lord Quill."

"I was on that side once, Daniel. And you had your chance with me. You chose this inane fight with your brother, not me."

"I tire of you. What is it that you want, Arcadis?"

My eyebrows creased and my red eyes sizzled with flames. I got mad at his disrespect, but bit my tongue. It took a second to calm down.

"Can't do much on that side either, can you?" Daniel laughed.

I smiled and then winked at him. "I can make sure the guards visit you nightly if you get my drift."

"You can't do that!" Daniel said with concern.

"Of course I can. I am the son of Lord Quill. They will do anything I ask."

"But your mother wouldn't allow it."

I laughed out loud. "Don't you get it? I saved your puny ass from my mother. She wanted you to be put on trial. I asked her not to. You'll be reconditioned like the rest of your crew."

He leaned on his chair in contemplation. "I still won't answer the question you had Rosinda ask me."

It was my turn to contemplate. Daniel knew something. The soul trees told me they provided him with a little information. I wondered if I threw some words around if he would react to them.

"Daniel, did you ever hear of clear magic?"

He seemed unfazed. "No. Are you making that up? What's clear magic? A normal human?"

Strike that one. "Did you ever hear of Toris, a mutual friend of Lord Quill?"

Again, Daniel shook his head no. "Why are you asking me irrelevant questions? I want to go to my cell now. You're boring me."

I ignored him. "How about Anala or Eos?" Bingo. It was a slight jerk of his head but I caught it. "Thanks for answering my question. What about Anala, the king of wizards? Is he planning a war on the warlocks and then us?"

He smiled as he stood. "I'll never tell." He walked back to the door and banged on it. I motioned to the guard to let him in. Before he walked through the door he said, "Nothing is as it seems, Arcadis, remember that."

So, Daniel didn't seek answers to the primaries' demise, or did he? What did Anala's impending war have to do with the sorcerers and the warlocks? Were they interrelated? Were they independent of one another?

The intercom blared, "Arcadis, please report to the Convocation chamber, thank you."

I stood up and hurried out the door. I walked into the infirmary since it was a shortcut and ran into Ciana. She looked haggard. I noticed a stain on her blue nurse's uniform and her hair had fallen out of her hat.

"What's wrong with you, Ciana? Had a bad day?"

"I've had better. I heard your name on the intercom, what's going on?"

"I don't know. I was talking to a prisoner and then the intercom went off."

"Have you had any more thought as to our discussion?" Ciana asked with a twisted smile.

I started to walk away. "No, but we can readdress it

soon. We may have to."

I heard her ask why as I left the infirmary. I didn't have time to chat. I have never before being summoned by an intercom. My mother usually communicates telepathically. I practically ran the rest of the way to the chamber.

When I got to the chamber, the door opened by itself. The two senior primary members were there, Arrake who wore his blue trench coat and his counterpart, Garnom, who wore his yellow trench coat. I did not see my mother. Alay burst through the door a few seconds later.

"I heard you being summoned by the loudspeaker and knew something was wrong. Where's our mother?"

I shrugged my shoulders. "I don't know. I was about to ask the other senior members."

We turned and faced them and bowed. They bowed back.

"My lieges, may I inquire where our mother is? If she

did not summon us here, then who did?"

Arrake spoke softly. "We did. It is an archaic form of communication, but it was imperative you knew the significance of our message."

"I'm sorry, but we don't. What message?"

Garnom's yellow trench coat opened slightly as he walked toward Alay and me. "Since you weren't privy to some of the Convocation's secret meetings, we need to be sure you'll both keep them quiet because what we're about to tell you may change the course of sorcerer history."

Melodramatic? Sure, but he got our attention. "That was in my oath when I became the Overseer, Sire."

"And I swear by my family's blood, I will not speak a word."

Both of them looked at each of us. "Know that you're in a sacred place and your word is your bond. If either one breaks that bond, you know the results," Garnom intoned.

Actually, it was only rhetorical since I possess unparalleled power, but I nodded.

Arrake came forward and offered us a chair. I was tired of sitting, but complied.

"Does either one know the mission Surla, Topec, and Roan went on?"

I looked to Alay and back to Arrake and Garnom. "No, they refused to tell me when I asked. Are they okay?"

"Where is our mother?" demanded Alay. I put my hand in hers and squeezed. It was a polite gesture to tell her to shut up. It worked.

"We will come to that, Alay. Be patient. First let me say that we just got word Surla, Topec and Roan are alive. We don't know if they're okay but at least they're alive." Arrake blew out some deep breaths before he continued. "The Chronicler and the two Regulators were on a secret mission. Their clandestine operation was to go to the wizards' realm and do reconnaissance. We heard the rumors of an impending war. A war we can't afford to lose. At first they sent some intel via a magical chute. Luckily we have one in the conference room so we were alerted to the message when it first arrived. The first message was brief. They explained they got there without incident and were scoping out the realm. The second message was more cryptic. "Be careful, nothing is as it seems!"

I threw my hands up in the air. "Do you know how many sorcerers have told me the same exact thing?"

Garnom raised an eyebrow. "Do you know what it means?"

I shook my head. "I haven't a clue and it's frustrating."

Arrake spoke up. "Regardless of its meaning, we received one last message approximately three hours ago. All it said was, 'We're in trouble.'"

I rubbed my chin in aggravation and noticed I needed a shave. Funny the things one thinks about when confronted with tension.

I noticed Alay bite her lower lip. She was dying to ask about our mother. She was a good warrior. She wanted information but her superior told her to wait. She was, but it was getting more difficult for her.

"Arrake, what does this have to do with our mother?" I looked to Alay as I spoke to let her know I was concerned too.

Arrake looked to Garnom who nodded. "After the third message, your mother grew very concerned and wanted to go and find them. We suggested she wait for you two but she refused. She has a tendency for stubbornness."

Alay was floored. "With all due respect, why did you let her?"

Garnom hesitated before speaking. "She overruled

us, pure and simple. She is the most senior member, we had to abide by her decision whether we agreed with it or not. Don't get us wrong, we strongly suggested she wait but she wouldn't listen. She was beside herself."

"Arcadis, does the book you absorbed say anything about this?" Arrake asked.

I searched the prophecy section, the stories, and anything that could relate to what was going on. "There is a small annotation in the prophecy section but it's extremely brief. It's almost like a riddle." My eyes went back and forth as I read and reread the sentence in my mind.

"Arcadis, what does the footnote say? Don't leave us hanging!" Alay shouted at me.

I understood her angst. I really did, but the sentence didn't make any sense. "We stood by the fire with our heads held high whilst we were extinguished."

The three of them looked at me. "What the hell does

that mean? And how does that reference the disappearance of everyone?" Alay said as she looked to me with crazed eyes.

I tried to sort out the confusion reigning in my mind. "It's hard to understand since the book took me to that sentence first in the prophecy section. I dismissed it and the book brought me to stories but none of them made any sense. None have to do with any of the keywords I used."

Alay stared at me with bewilderment on her face. "Arcadis, what are you talking about? What are keywords?"

I smiled. "Keywords are one or more words that describes what I am searching for."

"Example, please." She was growing impatient with me.

"Sure. If you wanted to find out about any skirmishes sorcerers have had, you put in the words skirmishes and sorcerers in the quantum magical computer. You would get many hits or sites devoted to those two words. The more words you put in, the more relevant it is what you're looking for."

Alay's blue eyes lit up in recognition. "Then what you did was put in more keywords to narrow your search, right?"

I nodded. "In my mind I put in Alexia, Topec, Roan, and Surla along with secret mission."

"And that sentence you recited is what came up?" Arrake asked with surprise on his face.

"Yes Sir, but in all honestly I have no idea what that means."

As I finished the last word of my sentence, the magical chute hummed. A piece of paper flew out and landed on the multi-colored carpet in the back of the room. Arrake retrieved it, read it, and came back to us.

Arrake showed Garnom the paper, looked at each

other and then to us. "We have a situation. Gather up the troops. I want every available sorcerer on the planet mobilized with twenty-four hours, Arcadis. As the Overseer it's your responsibility."

I bowed deeply. Alay was beside herself. "What does the paper say, Sir?"

Arrake handed the paper to her. I went to her side and read.

"We have your two Regulators, your Chronicler, and Madame Gildeon. If you want to see them alive, have the two other members of the Convocation come along with Arcadis." It was signed Anala, the king of the wizards.

Earlier I had mentioned very few things made me mad. I'll add this one to my list. No one, and I mean no one, abducts my mother or any other sorcerer and gets away with it. Yeah, I know they were in the wrong going over there but it was just reconnaissance, pure and simple. Go there, extract information, and come home. I was wondering if the wizards ever came over here?

Alay grabbed hold of my shoulders and shook me hard. "Arcadis, snap out of it! We're at war!"

So, for the second time in less than three months, we were at war. This time, however, it was personal.

To be continued...

Made in the USA
Charleston, SC
13 March 2015